ALSO BY PEG TITTLE

(fiction)

Gender Fraud: a fiction (forthcoming)
It Wasn't Enough
Exile
What Happened to Tom

(nonfiction)

Just Think About It
Sexist Shit that Pisses Me Off
No End to the Shit that Pisses Me Off
Still More Shit that Pisses Me Off
More Shit that Pisses Me Off
Shit that Pisses Me Off

Ethical Issues in Business:
Inquiries, Cases, and Readings (2nd ed.)
Critical Thinking: An Appeal to Reason
What If … Collected Thought Experiments in Philosophy
Should Parents be Licensed? Debating the Issues

IMPACT

IMPACT

PEG TITTLE

Magenta

Impact
© 2017 by Peg Tittle

pegtittle.com

First published 2020

978-1-926891-77-4 (print)
978-1-926891-78-1 (pdf)
978-1-926891-79-8 (ebook)

Published by Magenta

Cover design by Elizabeth Beeton and Peg Tittle

Formatting and interior book design by Elizabeth Beeton

Library and Archives Canada Cataloguing in Publication

Title: Impact / Peg Tittle.
Names: Tittle, Peg, 1957- author.
Identifiers: Canadiana (print) 20200194437 | Canadiana (ebook) 20200194445 | ISBN 9781926891774
   (softcover) | ISBN 9781926891781 (PDF) | ISBN 9781926891798 (EPUB)
Classification: LCC PS8639.I76 I47 2020 | DDC C813/.6—dc23

Thanks To...

Thanks to Meghan Murphy for Feminist Current and to all the intelligent women who engage in discussion there.

Thanks also to Lesley Baldwin for her enthusiasm and feedback.

1

A woman in her mid-twenties, wearing a simple blouse, skirt, and heels, waits in a room. A room that looks much like a cell, with its concrete floor, its concrete walls. She sits at a bare table. In an uncomfortable chair. She pulls a folder from her bag and lays it onto the table in front of her.

Two young men, both in their early twenties, both in prison garb—pity it's not bright pink instead of bright orange—are brought in by guards who sit them in the two chairs opposite her, then cuff their hands to the heavy rings set into the table. They stare at her.

"Who are you?" the first one finally asks.

She stares back. Disbelief on her face. "Who am I?"

"Yeah. Are you our new lawyer? Figures." He snorts with disgust.

He doesn't recognize her. She looks at the second one. He too— Do we really all look the same to you? Was it that simple? That horrible?

"I'm the waitress at Bud's Bar."

"Oh yeah," the first one says, after a moment, "you *do* look a little familiar."

"I'm the woman you assaulted. Sexually."

"No," he says. Casually.

"What do you mean 'No'?"

"We didn't sexually assault anyone. Don't know what you're talking about," he adds. Then looks at the second one. "Do *you* know what she's talking about?"

The second one shakes his head, grinning slightly. He'd like to cross his arms on his chest, but the shackles prevent it. Instead, he leans back as far as possible and spreads his legs far apart.

"That night, after closing," she—reminds? No, can't be. Insists.

"That was you? Okay, yeah ..." The first one smiles. As if remembering a rather pleasant day at the beach.

"But," he leans forward slightly and expresses genuine confusion, "you *wanted* it. Didn't she?" He turns to his buddy for confirmation. Because it wasn't really a question. "You remembered it wrong," he turns back to her, then leans back. "As we said in court."

No doubt. Victims were no longer required, forced, to face their assailants. In a public courtroom, no less. It was finally understood that the shame and intimidation could be too strong, too influential, especially in cases of domestic abuse—a misnomer if ever, since there was nothing domestic about having your body beaten beyond recognition by the man you (thought you) loved, the man you married *by choice*.

Some had objected to the change, reasoning that if the victim didn't have to look her or his assailant in the eye, she or he would feel free to embellish and fabricate.

But other arguments had prevailed, and now victims presented their testimony in closed chambers with only the judge, the prosecuting attorney, and the defendants' lawyers present. In some circumstances, a friend or family member was allowed to be present for emotional support. A recording was made and, if applicable, shown to the jury during deliberation. Testimony seemed as honest, as accurate, and not nearly as reluctantly given. There was talk of extending the change to all crimes.

"I didn't remember it wrong!" she says with some vehemence. "It was raining. You offered me a ride."

"And you said 'Yes,'" he says. Smugly. She is *so* naïve.

"To the ride! Not to sex!" Did they really think that consent to the one meant consent to the other? That when a woman accepted a ride—or an invitation to a party, or a drink, or dinner … Perhaps. After all, men defined … everything. She sighed.

"As *I* recall," the first one continues, "you said 'Yes, *please*'." He grins. Case closed.

And yet, here they were.

"Did you *hear* me say 'Yes'?" she asks. "To the sex."

"Didn't hear you say 'No,'" the first one snickers.

"But I did. Say 'No.' Several times. Loudly. Clearly."

"Didn't hear you," he says. Cheerfully. Definitively.

"Besides which," she ignores that, tries to ignore that, "it's not like the default is consent. You don't assume 'Yes' unless otherwise indicated. You assume 'No' unless otherwise indicated."

"Well, maybe we can just agree to disagree about that," he smiles. It's such a patronizing smile.

She tries to ignore that as well.

"Do you figure you have the right to just walk into someone's house without an invitation? Walk down their halls, into their rooms … " She shuddered. Every time—   She'd have to move.

He doesn't respond. It was a stupid question. That was break and enter.

"Do you think the rules are 'It's okay unless the person says it's not'?" she persists.

Again, he doesn't respond.

"Then what makes you think you have the right to come into my *body* without an invitation?"

They refuse to accept the analogy. She knew they would. A woman's body isn't a house. It's public property. That was part of why contraception and abortion were … issues.

Of course, she doesn't accept the analogy either. Her body wasn't her house. It was her. And after such a … violation, she couldn't just move.

"So, what, we have to *ask* now?" He stares at her in disbelief.

What? She stares at *him* in disbelief. "Yes!" Why was that so ... objectionable?

Ah. To ask for permission is a sign of weakness.

"Then again," she reconsiders, "no. Because if you have to ask whether a woman wants you, she probably doesn't. If she wants you, she'll move *toward* you, rather than away from you. For starters." How clueless were these guys?

And then it occurs to her. Neither one of them had probably ever made love. Or even made *like*. They had never engaged in simple, mutual pleasuring.

So they honestly *didn't* know. They genuinely thought this was the way it was supposed to be. Because it was all they'd ever seen. In the porn they no doubt watched. It was all they'd ever heard about. From their bragging buddies.

Why is rape something to brag about?

Even if they'd gone to a prostitute— Most are raped while on the job.

What these guys needed were a few sessions with a sex therapist.

Absent love, or even friendship, *genuine* friendship, between young men and women, that might lead to affectionate sexual interaction ...

But the male-female divide was so great now—walk into any toy store—it was nearly impossible to cross over and just *talk* to someone on the other side. Surely a prerequisite. What would they talk about? All they knew about the other, all they'd been told, by television, by advertisements …

Worse, all they knew about the other's sexuality, informed not just by porn, but also, even, by the ubiquitous pop music saturating their lives, pumping them full of sexualized energy—it was a far cry from the Pointer Sisters singing about a slow hand …

'Course even back then, did *men* listen to the Pointer Sisters? They laughed at Barry White.

"We didn't mean to hurt you," the second one speaks up. "We just meant to have a little fun."

What? She stares at him. Surely they've seen the photographs. (Though even absent physical injury …) Their lawyer must have presented that evidence during a pre-trial meeting. The prosecutor would surely have presented that evidence during the trial. Maybe they had their eyes closed. Their heads stuck in the sand.

She opens the folder and spreads the eight-by-tens onto the table in front of them. Like tarot cards.

"Does that look like fun? For me?" she has to add.

The first one glances at the photographs, then looks up at her. He shrugs. He has no idea what she considers fun. It's not really his concern, is it.

The second one's eyes widen before he looks away.

She repeats her question. "Does that look like I'm having fun?"

No, of course not. When people, almost always men, said 'We were just having fun,' what they meant was 'We don't want to be held responsible for what we did' or 'We didn't think it through.'

"Sorry," the first one shrugs. "Is that what you want to hear? Is this one of those victims' rights things? Are you here to tell us what bad boys we are?" He laughs and grins at his friend. Who grins back.

"No, I'm here to ask why." It was another change. These meetings, these confrontations, between victim and perpetrator, were permitted as part of the process. Any recommendations, by the victim, regarding sentencing, would be taken into consideration.

"Why did you rape me?" She asks the question.

"Because we could," the first one says. The second one giggles. Sort of.

This is all just a big joke to them. *She* is just a big joke to them.

One of the guards happens to pass by the door, so she signals to him. She needs a break.

*

"We thought you were okay with it," the second one said, perhaps a little too eagerly, as soon as she returned. "We thought you wanted it. It wasn't rape," he insisted. "It was just—sex."

She selected one of the photographs from the folder. "You thought I wanted—this?" She stood, to lean across the table and shove it in his face. "Why in god's name would you think *anyone* would want this?"

"Okay, maybe we, maybe *he*," he nodded to his buddy, "got a little carried away, but …"

His buddy smirked.

"Why would you think I wanted *any* of it?" she asked. Still standing. Still very much standing. "Why would you think I wanted some guys I don't even know to stick their dicks into me? At all?"

"But you *know* us! We're regulars!"

Well, that was true. She sat down. It was partly why she'd accepted the ride. They *were* regulars. And they seemed like nice guys. In fact, she thought they were students at the university. None of which, now, seemed to vouch for their character, their morality.

"That's not—that's not *knowing* you. And even if I *did* know you, that doesn't mean I want to have sex with you."

"But you're always smiling at us," the second one said. With what seemed to be genuine confusion.

"It's my *job!*" she protested. It was every woman's job. To smile at men. To appease them. To make them feel good. But then—
  Damned if you do …

And no wonder men didn't like it when women *didn't* smile.

"I was just being *friendly!*" She saw that she had to spell it out. "When a woman is friendly toward you, that doesn't mean she wants to have sex with you!" Were they so blind to nuance, to subtlety, to the whole *spectrum* of social engagement?

Perhaps. Thanks to cell phones and social media, society seemed to be devolving, moving backwards, from complexity to simplicity. Texting prevented full expression. Emoticons were essentially pictograms.

Men in particular seemed insensitive to … communication. She was going to say they weren't as good with words as women, then she was going to say they weren't as good with body language …

It would make things so much easier if we were open and clear, if we didn't have such a taboo about *talking* about *sex*. Though, oddly enough, words like fuck and cunt seem to come pretty easily to most people. Most men. So why isn't 'Do you want to have sex?' just as not-awkward?

Perhaps these two were just especially inept, misinterpreting social signals, failing to appreciate the multiple possibilities.

Or maybe there were no multiple possibilities for men. Men considered caressing to be foreplay. They considered kissing to be foreplay. In fact, everything but penetration was considered foreplay, was considered something inevitably leading *to* penetration. Because sex was *defined as* penetration, as penis-in-vagina. Women, on the other hand, might define a caress, or a kiss, or any of several other things, things other than penetration, as the desirable end point in and of itself.

Or maybe—maybe *she* was the one who didn't know the language. The thought startled her. Maybe *she* was the inept one. Maybe accepting one kind of invitation *did* mean accepting another. Now.

No, maybe men and women just used different languages. And there wasn't a word for 'no' in their language. Not that could be spoken by a woman.

"You didn't scream," the second one said. Trying to explain.

"I'm not a screamer. I use my words. And I did say 'No.'"

And actually, she did scream. When the first one—

"'No means yes, yes means anal,'" the first one said. And laughed. "Didn't you get the memo? Came from Yale even."

So he *did* hear her. Say 'No'.

"I also said 'STOP!' and 'GET OFF ME!' Tell me, what part of 'STOP!' and 'GET OFF ME!' didn't you understand?"

"We thought you were just—"

"Did I *look* like I was just—   What, bluffing? Kidding?" How could they know? They didn't look at her. Not really.

"You didn't fight back."

"I did so! I tried to push you off me. I tried to get out from under you."

He shrugged.

"And anyway, why should I *have* to fight back? Victims of other kinds of assault don't have to prove they resisted or that they didn't consent."

"Well yeah. Because no one in their right mind would consent to be beaten up." He laughed.

She stared at him. Waiting. In vain.

"We didn't think you meant it," the second one said.

Right. Men never took women seriously. Why should this be any different? What we say, what we do— None of it *means* anything. Certainly not anything important.

"Didn't you notice that I suddenly went still?" She'd hoped that that would minimize the injuries. If she stopped moving, stopped struggling—

"Yeah," the first one said. "We just figured you were frigid or something."

She considered that.

"Okay, and what does that mean? Doesn't it mean a woman doesn't enjoy sexual intercourse?" Or that you're not doing it right. Or that she's just not into you. "So ... wouldn't that make you stop?"

He shrugged.

She sighed. Whether or not a woman enjoys sex is irrelevant. We have vaginas, they're meant to have penises shoved in them, and especially if they've had penises shoved in them before, well, what's the big deal. Though they hadn't mentioned that yet.

And if the woman *hasn't* had a penis shoved in her vagina before, then, what, they were doing her a favour? Helping her out? Breaking her in?

She couldn't wrap her head around the logic.

Because there was none.

Or there was. And it was just so—

"Look, we thought you liked it," the second one tried again.

"Most women do," the first one took over. "You pretend you don't, but deep down you do."

"Most women like *rape?*"

He nodded. "I know for a fact that you like it when we hold you down, when we use force." There. Let her deal with *that*.

She doubted he knew *anything* for a fact. It was just the way some people, mostly men, talked. It made them appear knowledgeable. Presenting opinion as fact was how people, typically men, achieved and maintained their status as authorities, experts, fonts of wisdom … 'I know for a fact' just meant 'I'm guessing it's true.' Or 'I hope it's true.'

"It's a turn-on. Admit it." He was so smug.

She ignored the challenge. "And you know this because?" Because—wait, 'Most women'? She wondered how many …

He rolled his eyes. It was common knowledge, wasn't it.

"I want to be sure I understand you. You think most women like *this?*" She presented the photographs again. He refused to look.

"Oh no, you don't get to turn away," she said angrily. "LOOK!" She stood up, reached over, grabbed his hair, and forced him. To look. "LOOK AT WHAT YOU DID TO ME!"

He tried to pull away. Couldn't, really.

A guard appeared at the door, glanced inside, then stepped back, away from the small window.

She let go. Couldn't stand touching him.

"You did this to me! And this! And this!" She pointed to the photographs, one at a time. "Can you honestly tell me you thought I'd *like* it? Would *you* like it?"

He didn't answer.

"Then why do you think *I'd* like it?" She sat back down. Suddenly exhausted.

"You women like this sort of thing!" he insisted.

"'You women'? You've done this to other women? And they liked it? How did you know? When they struggled, you thought that meant they were having fun? When they begged you to stop? When they cried? When they screamed, you thought that meant they were enjoying it? And then when they just lay there, limp, hoping to get out of it alive, you thought they were having a good time?"

No response.

"Yes, many women moan during sex and cry out when they have an orgasm. Can you honestly not tell the difference between those moans and cries and *my* moans and cries?"

And that's when she knew for sure.

"You've never had sex," she said. "Real sex. Good sex. Sex with a woman who wanted it. Neither one of you. You don't *know* what happens when a woman has an orgasm."

The first one snorted.

She anticipated. "A woman who's not acting in a porn film. You know they're acting, right?"

Oh my god. They didn't know.

"You thought porn was real?" She stared at them. How stupid were they? "They're actors! Following a script! The director *tells* the woman to pretend she likes it. *Pretend.* Understand? It's *make-believe.*"

All of their knowledge about sex was based on make-believe. Certain men's fantasies.

And why do certain men fantasize about raping, about hurting and humiliating, women?

"Even prostitutes are acting," she said. Just in case. "They're saying and doing whatever they think will make them the most money.

"Many of them are acting for their lives. If they don't keep their customers satisfied, their employer, their pimp, will punish them. Hurt them. Horribly.

"In fact, many of them are actual prisoners. They've been kid-napped. Specifically to be bought and sold. Against their will. Ever hear of sex trafficking? Prostitution rings?

"They've been told what to wear, what to say, what to do. It's all an act."

"Oh, I'm pretty sure they're enjoying it," the first one grinned knowingly.

She just stared at him. And her whole body sighed into her chair. Because he would never acknowledge that he was complicit in a slave trade. That he *enjoyed* the enslaved.

And because quite apart from that, prostitution institutionalized the idea that men have a right—at least an economic right—to women's bodies. The idea that sex is a female service. As Brownmiller pointed out.

"Then you're easy to fool," she finally said. Because you're not interested in facts. You're not interested in truth.

She doubted they watched any erotica. She doubted they even *knew* about erotica. Because the erotica industry couldn't compete with the porn industry. Hell, not even the NFL could compete with the porn industry.

And why is that?

The closest they could come would be to watch some of the steamier scenes in chick flicks. So never gonna happen.

"You've never even *seen* consensual sex, have you. You've never seen two people make love. Say, a man and a woman, caressing each other, lingering with their hands on each other's body, kissing, touching, stroking, each of them getting more excited, until eventually, it might take half an hour, but that's okay because it feels so good, eventually the woman comes, usually because the man has been tickling her clitoris in a crazy-making way, and then the man enters her, and moves in and out, sometimes slowly, sometimes quickly, and sometimes she comes again in the time it takes for him to come, and then they lay together, lazily, tangled up in each other, languidly, with such …"

Both of them were just— Staring at her. The second one had his mouth slightly open.

"And you'll probably never *have* consensual sex," she muttered then. "You'll probably never make love."

The first one was, she had noticed, rather good-looking by contemporary standards. Which was initially a bit puzzling. Surely he didn't have to rape. But as one of the beautiful people, he would have received, throughout his life, better jobs, better pay, more credit, more attention … And those to whom much is given expect that much, and more. That is, he felt entitled. To whatever he wanted.

And it was quite possible he didn't *want* real sex. He didn't *want* a real relationship with a woman; his relationships with men were more important. *Men* were more important.

"What makes you say that?" the second one asked. In a small voice.

"Well, because I can't imagine any— You're not— What's there about you to love?"

2

A week later, she was back in the room, back in the prison. Five minutes after her arrival, still a little unnerved to have gone through the rigorous security check and then to have been escorted by an armed guard, the two men were again brought in and shackled to the table.

"What I don't get is," the second one spoke up as soon as he entered the room, "if you're not looking for it, why do you all go around looking like Miley Cyrus?"

What? She *didn't* go around looking like Miley Cyrus. Though, she had to admit, many of the younger women seemed to. They'd bought the same shit these guys had bought.

"With your short skirts and your fuck-me shoes," the first one added.

"Well, I can't speak for other women, but *I* was wearing a skirt because it's my uniform," she replied.

"And now?" he asked.

He was right. Even then, there, she was wearing a skirt. And heels. Not so-called 'fuck-me' heels, but perhaps men couldn't distinguish between those and regular heels. If they couldn't even distinguish between one woman and the next.

So, actually, she *could* speak for other women. Wearing a skirt or a dress, and heels, a bit of make-up, a bit of jewelry—it was just normal, just convention. It was expected.

And why is showing your legs expected? Of women?

She dressed that way to look nice.

Right, but what does 'look nice' mean? Didn't she look okay just as she was?

She wanted to be attractive.

But what does wearing skirts as opposed to pants have to do with looking attractive? 'Looking attractive' could only mean, then, 'looking *sexually* attractive.' Because the difference was showing your legs. And legs, women's legs, were, had become, sexualized.

And, if it was a tight skirt, a sheath skirt, the difference was restricting your movement.

And *that* had become sexualized?

And heels made your legs appear more … shapely. Longer, essentially. Because … why were long legs more sexually attractive? Ah. Long legs accentuated the eye's journey to the apex, the prize, the point of entry.

Valian was right: sexualizing our appearance had become normalized. It had become just as much a uniform— It was expected. Almost required. Even feminists were wearing make-up now. Well, so-called feminists.

Even so. Dressing to be sexually attractive didn't mean she wanted to attract—yes, it did. It meant exactly that. Attractive. Attracting. Attract. Bring to.

Well, maybe for a look. Not necessarily for intercourse. Certainly not for violence.

And she certainly didn't want to attract *all* men.

But how could she be selective? With her appearance. It was impossible.

So she *was* attracting all men, then rejecting most of them. What an inefficient way to—to what? Find a mate? Why was she doing that with appearance anyway? Didn't she want a mate to be someone who liked her for what, for who, she *was?*

Well, yes, if we're talking about a long-term partner. But if we're talking about just a hook-up, just a one-night stand … Then why was she making herself sexually attractive *as a matter of routine.* Here. Now. Wouldn't she do it just when she went to parties or whatever?

They were right, she realized. It was, at least, part of the big picture. The cultural norm was that women should look a certain way, a way that emphasizes their sexuality, a way that turns men on a bit, a way that makes men think they're available to them. When she conformed to that norm, she was, to some small extent, complicit. She didn't tease, but yes, she tried to be attractive. She tried to attract.

Then again, if she intended to turn down most of the men she attracted—because no, she didn't want to have sex with most men—*wasn't* that teasing?

"Well?" the first one challenged.

"I'm thinking," she replied. "You should try it some time."

He rolled his eyes.

But the make-up, that was just to make you look younger, generally speaking. To get rid of the wrinkles and the other imperfections that developed as one aged.

Imperfections.

It was a little disturbing, now that she thought about it. That evidence of age was considered an imperfection. That youth was considered … preferable.

But it was true: younger bodies *were* more physically attractive. And therefore more sexually appealing? Wait, did that necessarily follow?

More importantly, did it *have* to mean endorsing *pedophilia*?

Because women shaved their legs. Yes, but just to make them smoother.

And their armpits. Yes, but again—

And now their crotches. The result *was* a prepubescent look. Yes, but it also just made things … more accessible.

She sighed. It was complicated. Worse, it was ambiguous.

And then something else occurred to her. The time and energy it all took. The shaving, the plucking, the make-up, the hair … Was that part of it? Women were supposed to spend a lot of time and energy attracting men? Pleasing men? What for? Seriously. Because what have they done for us lately?

Under the table, she slipped off her shoes. Only partly because her feet hurt.

And that's when *that* occurred to her: women were also supposed to be willing to endure pain if it pleased men.

There has been more research on male sexual pleasure than on female sexual pain. Five times more. One in three women feel pain during vaginal penetration; two in three, during anal penetration. They just don't tell their partners. Women *often* ignore or downplay their own distress so as not to upset others, typically men. All this, why? Because, as Loofbourow put it, "We live in a culture that sees female pain as normal and male pleasure as a right."

"You all go around looking like hos," the first one summarized, impatient, "then cry rape when we treat you like one."

What? It took her a moment. "Prostitutes don't want to be raped."

Quite apart from they couldn't distinguish between prostitutes and women who'd just made themselves sexually attractive? Maybe not. It was, after all, just a matter of degree.

She recalled picking up a guy at a bar one night. She'd begun the conversation, she'd made the suggestion. He'd thought she was a prostitute. Apparently the only women who could initiate a sexual encounter were prostitutes. Denied that active role, no wonder consent could be troublesome. Maybe for a long time 'no' *had* meant 'yes'. Because 'yes' meant 'I'm a prostitute.'

And if the screaming and struggling was also just a matter of degree, expressions of protest too similar to expressions of acquiescence—no, she didn't believe they were that similar. But maybe that was just her?

No. Because what about 'Stop!' and 'Get off me!'

And, the thought occurred to her, the difference wasn't just a matter of degree in appearance. The prostitute expected payment in cash, then and there. Other women expected … to have their way paid. For the night. For the rest of their lives. She sighed.

No wonder they have such contempt for us.

Then again, not all women.

And then again, men often *demand* such dependence. They often insist on paying our way. Their masculinity depends on it.

Or does their subsequent use of our bodies depend on it?

At the same time, they seem to resent our dependence.

And they often become enraged when we become, or are, *in*dependent. When we leave them or don't need them in the first place.

Go figure the logic.

"All women are hos," the first one said. With such disgust.

Yes. That was it. It wasn't a case of mistaken identity. Because even when women were completely covered up, head to toe, in burkas, men hurt them. Because even women over fifty, over sixty, over seventy, were raped.

And the logic, again— They demand sexiness, and then, when we comply—or not, they insult, call us sluts. Hos.

"Even if my appearance *did* indicate that I wanted sex," she backed up and made a turn, "that doesn't mean I'm going to go through with it. I may want to eat a whole carton of ice cream. Doesn't mean I'm going to. And if you offered me a whole carton of ice cream, I'd say 'No thanks.'"

She realized then that that was another distinction they couldn't make. The distinction between what they wanted and what they did. They just did whatever they wanted. Like two-year-olds.

"But you didn't *offer* me anything. You just assumed. You made the decision for me. As if you know best. What I want and what I don't want. Which wants I'll satisfy and which ones I won't. Who the hell do you think you are?" she glared at them. "You don't know shit! About me!"

They stared at her.

"Or is it that you think women in general are unable to decide, unable to speak, for themselves?" She continued to glare at them. "We're not stupid. And we're not children."

Despite what so many movies, certainly the ones these guys watch, say.

And not just movies, she thought with despair. In the real world, how many positions of power, of responsibility, are occupied by women? Somewhere between 20 and 30 per cent. And it's the *other* 70 to 80 percent that gets media coverage. When media coverage is granted. To women. So no one sees, no one knows about, even that meager 20 to 30 percent.

"On the contrary, I can—and did—speak for myself. You ignored me."

No surprise there.

So maybe— Maybe we've been looking at the wrong thing. *For the wrong thing.* We should be looking not for the presence of consent, but for the presence of *coercion.* MacKinnon once said, in *Are Women Human?*, that coercion has been hidden. Behind consent.

Still.

"Even if a woman *does* ask for it— Suppose she's drunk or for some other reason isn't acting in her own best interests— Are you obliged to do it? Might you not have a moral obligation to refuse? Take the higher road?"

"Okay, look, maybe we made a mistake," the second one said. It was intended as a peace offering.

A mistake? No. Despite the porn, despite the ambiguities, she couldn't quite believe they really thought that what they did was sex.

She thought maybe they really preferred rape. To sex.

Is that because that's the way they're built, biologically, or because that's the way they've been made, socially? Studies suggest that exposure to porn eventually makes power, dominance, even violence, the only way to sexual arousal, to satisfaction. But maybe they're wired that way from the get-go. Maybe sex, regular sex, for men, has always been all about power and dominance. That could explain why so many of them have been uncomfortable with her on top. Rape was also about power and dominance. Therefore.

And maybe they know porn's fake. And maybe they just don't care. Grisham's *The Appeal* had opened her eyes on this matter. She'd realized that for most men, power matters. And she'd come to realize that truth didn't matter. She'd also realized that money was important, because it could buy things. But she hadn't put it all together the way Grisham had. Money can also buy friends. Not *real* friends, but that doesn't matter. What matters is what those 'friends' say and do. *Whether it's sincere or not, whether it's motivated by genuine affection or personal gain, doesn't matter.* So the women are acting? They're just *pretending* to like it? Doesn't matter. What matters is that men have so much power over them, they can *make* them *say* they like it. *That's* the turn-on. The power.

And *that's* why so many rapists insist their victims say they like it. Not to assure them that what they're doing is consensual, but to prove that they have that power. The more obvious the lie—that is, the greater the pain—the greater their power.

"Yeah," the first one chimed in. "It was a mistake. Get over it."

Get over it? She turned to look at him. *Get over it?* She started to bring out the photographs again. But doing so would just show the physical trauma. Which, yes, eventually she would get over.

"You shouldn't've gotten into the car," the second one said, returning to the astonishing and indefensible overgeneralization of consent.

"Oh it's *my* fault? *My* fault you raped me?"

Of course it was. Women were expected to take full responsibility for—what men do to them. Which required limiting their choices with regard to … everything.

"We were a little drunk, okay?" he added.

She stared at him. "So?"

He didn't elaborate. Of course not. He probably couldn't. How could he be so … stupid? *And* be a university student? Oh, well, no-brainer, as they say. This was introspection. Analysis of one's beliefs and behaviours. Not something that came with a university education. Especially if one was male.

"You think that *absolves* you?" she asked. "You think getting drunk releases you from responsibility? For whatever you do *while* drunk? Wouldn't that be convenient."

At least *she* hadn't been drunk or drugged. Though sometimes she wished she had been.

She remembered a video she'd seen showing a young man in close-up whispering to the viewer about what he was going to do to the woman in the background, who was passed out on the couch. He then goes to the woman and gently puts a pillow under her head and just as gently covers her with a blanket. What shocked her was that she was shocked. It was just a simple act of kindness. But—

"Works for me," he grinned.

She got up. She had to get out of there.

And although she left the room, there was no getting out of there. She knew that now.

3

A week later, she showed up again. She would continue to do so until she understood. The first time, she heard nothing but denial. The second time, excuse. What would it be this time?

"What, you've turned into a dyke?" The first one sneered.

"Why do you say that?" She was truly mystified.

"Your clothes."

She looked down at her sweatshirt, loose cotton pants, and track shoes. Yes, she had given all that some further thought. And had, obviously, come to several conclusions. But not that one.

"You think that any woman who doesn't wear a skirt and heels is a *lesbian?*" she asked. "Why would you think that?" Again, truly mystified.

No answer.

"You also think that any woman who *does* wear skirt and heels wants to have sex with every man, yeah?"

No answer.

"So," she put two and two together, "you think that to be a straight woman is to be sexually available to every man." It would explain why they felt entitled to her body. To avail themselves of it without asking. "So it's conceptually impossible to rape a straight woman."

They were silent. They hadn't followed the logic. Obviously Business students. No, that was unfair, she chided herself. Men of all stripes were notoriously lacking in logic. Logic was all about relationship. This *therefore* that.

"What if I *was* a lesbian?" she asked then. "Would what you did to me be rape *then?*"

"No, it would be teaching you a lesson," the first one laughed.

She ignored the laughter. Had to.

"What lesson?"

He couldn't say. Of course he couldn't.

It was called 'corrective rape' in some countries. And it was, absurdly, intended to convert the woman to heterosexuality.

"That I'm *supposed* to be available to all men?" She stared at them. "Why would you think *that?*"

No answer.

"I think you're lying," she said then. Flatly. "You didn't think I was okay with it, you didn't think I wanted it, you didn't think I liked it. You heard me say 'No.' You didn't think I was joking, you knew I meant it. You didn't just make a mistake. You knew full well you were raping me. So. Why?"

She looked pointedly at one and then the other.

The second one shrugged.

"That's not an answer!" She raised her hands—as if she could shake him out of his complacence. "Why did you do it?" She shouted the question.

Silence.

Answering a woman's question is emasculating. It's acceding to her request. Paying attention to what she wants. It was beneath them. Even so, she asked yet again.

"Why did you rape me?"

Had they been victims of violence? That was the theory. A theory. What goes around comes around. Violence is a learned behavior.

But no, what were the odds. That both of them had been victims of violence, that both of them had been, specifically, sexually assaulted.

Besides, she didn't buy it. *She* now had been assaulted, sexually, but she had no inclination, now, to go and assault, sexually assault, someone else. None whatsoever.

The first one shrugged. "It's not like you're married or anything." He looked pointedly at her hand.

It took her a moment to connect the dots. "What, once I'm married, that would mean I'm off-limits? Because then I belong to another man? Whereas until then— I'm not a piece of property!" she said sharply.

But that is, after all, how it began. 'To have and to hold' was a legal phrase that referred to property ownership. Not physical affection. And until 1983—*1983!*—husbands could legally rape their wives. Because, after all, they owned them.

The ring? Remnant of the shackle.

The name change? Indicative of the transfer of ownership from father to husband, from one male to another.

How a man feels when his wife has sex with another man? Not sadness, for the loss of love. No. Rage. At the theft.

Then she saw another—

"Do you know what a false dichotomy is?" she asked them.

Of course they didn't.

"You're assuming that I'm available either to only one man or to all men. There is a third option. And a fourth."

They stared at her. Incomprehension on their faces. That she might be completely unavailable had not occurred to them. Nor, apparently, that she might be available only to those she chose.

"It's just physical," the first one said then. Only slightly changing the topic. "Instinct. Basic needs and all that."

Right. The myth that supports porn, prostitution, rape. Because we must, we absolutely *must*, provide whatever men need.

"First, no, it's not a need."

Despite what his Psych 101 text would have said. Because it was probably written by a man. Who either wanted to believe that sex was a need or who mistook what was true of the whole for what was true of the parts. On a *species* level, yes, sexual intercourse is needed, for survival. *Of the species.* But on an individual level?

"You won't die if you don't have sex," she pointed out the obvious. "Oxygen, water, food, and a certain range of temperature are needs. Everything else is a want."

But saying you *need* something makes it so much harder for others to refuse to give it to you. Because needs are, well, things one *needs*—they're *required*. Needs take priority to wants.

But they aren't, therefore, entitlements.

"And even if it *were* a need, even if you *did* have to ejaculate in order to survive, there's nothing saying you have to do so inside a woman. Is there?"

Silence.

"So why not just jerk off when the desire overwhelms you?"

He snorted.

"What does that mean?" she asked.

"Seriously," she continued, when it seemed he'd thought she'd asked a rhetorical question, "I don't understand your response. What's snort-worthy of masturbation? Real men don't masturbate? Is there something insulting about doing it yourself, about not having to need a woman to do something? I would think it'd be the other way around. Real men *don't* need women. Isn't that right?"

Surprise flickered across his face. He hadn't considered it that way.

"So I guess it's not about sex. The need for sex. Because I'm sure there are, or could be, sexual aids, moist, warm, tight somethings, that would feel as good, probably even better. So … what *is* it about?"

No response. Were they truly that oblivious?

Perhaps. She'd read that when young women in a university classroom described what they did to avoid rape—be aware of your surroundings at all times, choose carefully when and where you go alone—the young men in the class "gaped in astonishment".

"It's about the need for dominance," she told them. "So-called need. Because you don't need dominance either. You won't die if you're not in power over someone. Will you?"

No response. No surprise.

If anything, sex was a *social* need. For men. A socially *constructed* need. *Real* men had sex, real men *wanted* sex, *lots* of sex. Their identity *as men* depended—*depended*—on having sex. And if they had to use force, all the better.

"You *want* dominance. You *want* to have power over. At least, over women. But why?"

No response. My god, it was like having a conversation with molasses.

"Because that's what *real* men— You have to keep saying 'I'm better than you, I'm one-up on you, I'm higher in the hierarchy than you.' Because … if you don't keep saying it, what, you'll forget?" She laughed.

The first one's hands curled into fists. She saw that. It actually looked involuntary. Atwood famously said men are afraid women will laugh at them. Whereas women are—

"No, because if we don't keep saying it, *you'll* forget!" the first one spat out.

Okay, good comeback, she had to give him that.

"That's why you didn't just assault me, why you didn't just beat me up. That's why you did it *sexually*. You wanted to send a message to me, to women as a group. You wanted to express your feelings toward women as a group."

"I don't have *feelings* toward women as a group."

She rolled her eyes.

Then continued. "So you raped me to put me in my place. To remind me that I'm subordinate to you."

She took the absence of denial to mean confirmation. It was as good as she was going to get.

"And what makes you think *that?*"

He snorted again. It passed for 'I don't know.'

"The fact that I'm a waitress? Because I'm also a student."

The second one's eyes widened.

"What, waitresses can't go to university? University students can't be waitresses?"

She turned back to the first one.

"But that's irrelevant, isn't it. Even if I were a *professor*, you'd think I was subordinate to you. That I'm *female* trumps whatever else I might be. And *why* again are females subordinate to, inferior to, males?"

They had no answer. Of course, they didn't.

*

When she returned, she decided to try another approach. "How would you feel if *you* were raped?" Apparently empathy wasn't one of their strong suits. No surprise, really. We don't encourage our little boys to feel. Let alone to think about what others feel. In fact, we *discourage* it. Big boys don't cry. So the tears of others? Not really on their radar.

"It's different," the first one said.

"Agreed. But—"

"You're used to it."

What? Not the difference she had in mind.

She supposed he was trying to say that a vagina was built for penetration but an anus wasn't. Where to begin? Perhaps with the point that having a particular capacity doesn't necessarily mean one wants to use that capacity. But no, one's wants, at least *her* wants, were irrelevant. They'd established that.

"I assure you, I am not used to this." She spread the photographs in front of them again.

"And even if I were—even if I *were* hurt this badly on a regular basis, how does that make it okay?"

They seemed to have no understanding of ethics. No idea about how to determine right and wrong. And it would take years to— Not her job. Not her responsibility.

So whose responsibility was it? Why were so many men apparently so ethically-challenged? Because being concerned about right and wrong makes you a wuss, a boy scout, a sissy. How, when—*why* did ethics become a sign of weakness, childishness, effeminacy?

"Well, you *should* be used to it. It's all you're good for." Again he spat the words out.

"*It's all we're good for?*" She couldn't believe what she was hearing. She could give them a few lessons in women's history. No doubt it would be the first time they'd hear that *a woman* discovered pulsars. 'Course, they may not know what pulsars are. Okay, she could tell them that *a woman* invented Kevlar. But no, it wasn't her job to educate them. Women got suckered into that far too often. We are not responsible for them. It is not our duty to make them better people. She had to remind herself that that wasn't why she was here. She was here merely to understand. Them.

Besides, it wasn't that he thought that that was all they were good for because he was unaware of women's achievements. He didn't consider women capable of achievements.

When he looked at a woman, all he saw was a sexual ... thing. A cunt.

When he'd first come into the room, he hadn't recognized her. This wasn't personal. Just the opposite. It was impersonal. That is to say, he didn't even consider women to be persons. She was just in the wrong place at the wrong time. Any pers—any female, any *cunt*, would have done.

"I'm a person," she said. "Just like you. Well, not just like you. Not anything like you, actually. What I mean is I'm not just—
   Women are not females. We are human beings who happen to be female. Consider it an adjective, not a noun."

Their faces were blank.

She tried again. "We're not women, ladies, girls, chicks, birds, cows, bitches, whores, cunts. We're people. Just ... people."

Still blank.

"Okay, let's try this. Tell me about some of the women in your life."

"What do you mean?" the second one spoke up.

"I mean *tell* me about them. What are their likes, their dislikes? What are their dreams, their aspirations? What do they think about?"

Silence.

They didn't know. She sank back into her chair. They truly didn't see 'person' when they saw 'female'.

Perhaps she shouldn't be so surprised. Her own father didn't seem to distinguish— There was Mike, her brother, and then there were 'the girls', her and her sister. They were undifferentiated. In his mind.

"We really *aren't* people to you," she said, slightly amazed. "None of us. We're just ... we really are just walking cunts. The only thing about us that registers with you is our sex. We have breasts. We must have a vagina. So we can be fucked. End of story."

"What more *is* there?" the first one laughed.

"Well," she said, and knew as soon as she started that it was a mistake, "I'm actually a *grad* student at the university. I just waitress on the weekends because I don't make enough as a teaching assistant to pay for rent, tuition, my bus pass—"

"In what, women's studies shit?"

"No," she said levelly. "But I'm curious as to why you consider women's studies to be shit. Oh wait. Because everything to do with women is shit. Because ... Help me out here. Oh wait. You can't." Said not so levelly. She glared at him. At his inability, his refusal, to think.

"All right," he seemed to switch a gear, "you've had your fun. Guard!" He looked toward the door, then back at her. "Play time's over."

At that moment, she—well, she already despised him. But the patronizing tone, the implied trivialization of what she was doing—and he was younger than her! It was unfuckingbelievable how men could do that. And of course, they'd been doing that to her all her life. Infantilizing her. All her life.

Perhaps because the more they infantilized others, the more mature they themselves felt.

No guard appeared at the door. She smiled.

"You are utterly and absolutely … unaware," she continued, truly a little amazed. "You have no idea why you think the way you do, why you act the way you do. You've avoided introspection all your life, so you have no self-knowledge whatsoever. You're just a robot. Completely bereft of consciousness."

He tried to shrug off her criticism. Failed. His shackles dragged across the table as if he was getting ready to—

"If you only had a brain." She leaned back in her chair, crossed her arms, and stared at him.

"GUARD!" He screamed. No fucking way he was going to put up with this.

And yet, he wouldn't've been able to say why. Why he wasn't going to put up with this. He was angry, yes. But *why* was he so angry?

Even if he *did* know, even if he *could* say, he wouldn't. Because explaining something to a woman is considered a favour. Not an obligation. Let alone a duty.

Though of course he wouldn't be able to provide that explanation either. For his behaviour.

So much sexism. So much of it unconscious.

They don't *intentionally* keep us out of the loop, she realized. They don't intentionally hoard the power that knowledge provides. They don't *intentionally* take the lion's share of … everything.

Nor, apparently, did they *intentionally* rape us.

*

"Look, you're making too much of this," the second one said when she returned. Trying to … appease? By telling her she was exaggerating the importance, the consequences, of what they'd done to her? "You're overthinking it," he added. Helpfully.

Hm. She was overthinking it. Would he have said that if she hadn't told them she was a student? How quickly they can turn the other's advantage into a disadvantage. Damned if you do.

But no. She'd heard that a lot. Usually from men. Men who didn't know anything about her.

Because any thinking at all would expose their lack of thought. The absence of reason, intent, consciousness.

Or the psychopathology. That is male. That is, masculinity.

"It's just what guys do!" There was exasperation in his voice. Pity, no despair. "Happens every day," he added.

Well, he was right about that. But he seemed to think that that made it inevitable.

"Yeah, it's no big deal," the first one piled on. "Everybody does it."

"Everybody does *not* do it," she said. "Besides, so what? At best, that's an explanation, not a justification. Do you know the difference?"

No response.

"I didn't think so. An explanation is simply that: it's something that explains why or how something else happens. A *justification* is a line of reasoning that explains why the something is okay. Typically, *morally* okay. So unless you're saying that you did it *because* other people do it— *Are* you saying that?" she had to ask. "Do you do what you do because other people do it?" She looked at one and then the other. "Do other people run your lives?"

The first one turned his gaze to the ceiling. Maybe she'd get the hint.

"Regardless, it's an inadequate response. Because many men have *not* raped a woman."

But one in five have. One in three college-aged men say they would if they thought they could get away with it. And okay, that's not even half, let alone most. But if you interact with, say, only a dozen young men during the course of a day, you can infer that four of them would rape you if they could get away with it. Every day, four of the men you talk to would like to hurt you.

And one in three is enough to make it normal, she thought. So these two, they weren't sick, they weren't broken, they hadn't been abused. *Or they were all of the above, and that was the norm.* For men. To *be* sick, broken, abused. God knows, we raise them to be less than full human beings.

And because of that, it was the norm for women as well. To be sick, broken, abused. To consider themselves to have fulfilled their potential if they were attractive.

"You put up with it," the first one said. Giving an explanation? A justification? "I wouldn't."

She looked at him.

"How would we *not* put up with it?" she asked. "What would *you* do?"

"Carry."

She thought about that. He was right. Absolutely right. If packs of wolves were roaming the streets and thousands, *tens* of thousands, of men were attacked every year, they'd organize an extermination campaign. They'd shoot every wolf on sight. Whether or not it, individually, had shown signs of violent behaviour.

"But how would you prove that you shot in self-defence?" Because it was more like living in an occupied country.

He shrugged.

"So your 'not putting up with it' wouldn't work, would it." She stared at him. Because people in occupied countries don't get a trial. Let alone a fair trial.

He didn't say.

"I think if you carried a gun, if you shot someone who grabbed you, his buddies would just take care of you." Odd euphemism. 'Take care of you.' Leave it to men to say exactly the opposite of what they meant.

"Kill you," she clarified. "Probably with your own gun. Just to make a point."

Silence.

"So I ask again. How would you not put up with it?" Because she really wanted to know.

4

Another week passed. She returned to the prison to meet with the men again.

When she entered the room, only the second one was there. She wasn't told why.

"So." She looked at him. He was a little less inflated without his buddy beside him. "You really believe women are just cunts? You really think we exist simply for you to fuck?"

He shrugged.

She waited.

"We thought you'd be easy points," he eventually said. A little apologetically. "We saw your boyfriend or whoever come out of your apartment in the morning sometimes … "

And there it was.

Wait—

"You live in my apartment building?" She thought they just knew her from the bar.

He nodded.

"And you thought what, if she's having sex with one man, she'll want to have sex with *every* man? Why would you think that?"

Because *men* want to have sex with every *woman*. Duh.

The ability to distinguish one's own desires from those of other people was considered a milestone in social development. Typically achieved in childhood.

"And—easy points?"

Must they turn *everything* into a competition? Sports, dance, cooking, travel, she thought of all the television shows ... even love, apparently. *The Bachelor* and its many spin-offs.

Which meant that every wife was a trophy. At minimum, a badge of respectability. An unmarried man, a bachelor, was considered immature, unsettled, unreliable. A bachelor would never become president. Of anything. All the men in upper management had wives. They had to.

Still. Everything?

"Oh, I get it," she said then. "Making everything a competition maximizes your chances of winning. *Something.* And you must win. Otherwise you're a loser." And there's nothing worse for a man to be.

Well, except a girl.

She looked at him. Searched his eyes for some ... some glimmer of ... "Don't you see you're a loser already, if you buy into this shit?"

He did. God help him, he did. A little bit. Now.

"Can't you just *enjoy* … anything?"

Then the rest of it fell into place.

"So I'm a—*a game piece* to you?"

Yes. That's exactly what she was. A piece. In their games. It's what all women were. Men competed with each other using women. Getting laid, having a girlfriend, getting married, having kids. All of it used women's bodies for points. We are, as Henstra put it in *The Red Word*, currency.

In fact … She remembered an episode of Sarkeesian's *Feminist Frequency* that included clips from popular video games: *Sleeping Dogs, Dishonored, Saints Row, Red Dead Redemption, Hitman, Assassin's Creed, Far Cry, Watch Dogs, Grand Theft Auto* … It was such an eye-opener. What she saw was sick. Truly sick.

In *Watch Dogs*, a man beats up a woman who has had the nerve to leave him. Administering first aid, calling paramedics, or even stopping to see if she's okay are not among the options available to the player. Apparently whether the woman lives or dies doesn't matter. The player *can* intervene, but if he intervenes too soon, the assault stops, and he gets no points. Better to wait until the woman is murdered and the man runs away, so the player can hunt him down for a fight. The woman is just a means to the player's end: winning a fight. She's just a game piece. Literally.

Bizarrely, the scene is repeated over and over. Talk about indoctrination.

And whenever a player wins, he gets a reward, often a 'cash' reward. Talk about reinforcement. The route to addiction.

In another game, when a female character—and every single one of them has huge breasts, a tiny waist, and huge buttocks—when the female character cries out for help and screams in pain, the male character says things like "Quiet, bitch, shut the fuck up!" and "You worthless whore, you're fucking pathetic!" In one case, the man says "Stinkin' whore, I'm going to cut you a new hole. You think I'm a joke?" (Had she laughed at the size of his penis? Oh well, then.) "Go on … laugh, bitch, laugh!" he says as he jabs a knife into her body again and again. "Damn it all," he adds when he's done, in an aggrieved voice, as if someone had just knocked over his bottle of beer. (Because what, she'd gone and died, and now he'd have no one, nothing, to fuck anymore?)

Who writes these things? she'd wondered. Men. Ordinary men.

In every case, as Sarkeesian notes, the woman's battered body is just swept away: women are not only commodified, as both motivator and reward, they are not only instrumental, and violable, they are also disposable. They are literally dragged behind a curtain. Where we can't see it. Her. Them. So many women are brutalized, to death, in video games.

"You can't just do what you did," she said quietly. To the man sitting in front of her. "You can't just turn off the game, finish your beer, then go to bed. You certainly don't get a cash reward for it," she added.

Porn was too mild a term for what she'd seen. Misogyny, too mild a term. The games were essentially animated snuff films. *Interactive* animated snuff films.

At the very least, they portrayed hate crimes with no pretensions to artistic or documentary value. Why were they even legal? Replace all the women with black-skinned people and make all the men white, and there's *no way* they would be allowed.

Let alone, she'd added to herself, replace all the women with men and all the men with women—though she couldn't imagine women— Actually, she could. Now. She imagined it every night.

Perhaps most horrible was that they were called *games*.

"Life isn't a video game," she followed up on her 'not a game piece' comment. "It's not even like tv. Well, tv made in Hollywood. Since that's probably the only tv you watch."

The problem used to be that almost every female character was young and pretty and existed for the man. She helped him. She made him feel important. She made him feel competent. She fell in love with him. She saved him from himself.

Now, almost every female character was sexualized. *Pornified.* She couldn't even watch *So You Think You Can Dance* anymore. (And the women there weren't even *characters* per se; nonetheless, they were surely pressured, by the choreographer and the costume designer …)

"The women you see on tv, they're acting. They're playing a part someone wrote for them, saying what the writer tells them to say, doing what the director tells them to do. You get that, right?" She'd made this point before, with regard to porn, but she wasn't sure it had sunk in.

Studies show that a lot of people can't tell the difference. Actors who play doctors are regularly approached on the street for medical advice. And *Grey's Anatomy* and the like didn't even engage our Neanderthal hindbrain like video games and porn did. So can we blame viewers for their mistaken belief?

Yes. Because studies also show that exposure to tv influences real-life attitudes and opinions, including those toward and about women. And no one forces people to expose themselves to tv. No one forces young men to spend hours playing those video games, to become addicted to the violence, to increase their threshold to violence, to become desensitized to violence toward women.

"Miley Cyrus isn't an actress," the young man sitting before her said.

"Sure she is. She's a performer. She's *performing* a role for fame and fortune. Though," she conceded, "she might be like that in real life too." Most celebrities weren't very educated. They certainly didn't spend much time reading and thinking about things. No surprise, as 'Hanakai Wren' said on *Feminist Current*, that their idea of liberation is twerking in public.

"We're not like that," she said. "Real women. We're not like the women on tv. We're not supporting characters in your life. We don't exist only in relationship to you. We have an independent existence. And you have no idea what I'm talking about," she saw the look on his face. "Okay, here's the simplified version: we do not exist for you. Let me repeat that. Women do not exist for men."

She wished that Canada and the States would require Hollywood to issue Bechdel ratings, as Sweden had done long ago. She was pretty sure that at the moment, almost every movie would fail the test. Which is to say that in almost every movie, there wasn't even a single conversation between two named women that wasn't about a man. It was an incredibly low bar. The movie didn't even have to have a major female character. Let alone one who was a feminist. It just had to have one conversation, it didn't even have to be a *long* conversation, that was between two women, who had names, that wasn't about a man.

The few movies that *did* pass the bar, she thought, were probably considered chick flicks. Which is to say they wouldn't be seen by, wouldn't have any influence on, any men.

"Yes, almost all of the women in movies and games are hot. Yes, almost all of the women in movies and games pay attention to the men. Yes, almost all of the women in movies and games want it bad. But, the women in movies and games *do not represent REAL women!* I repeat: real women *aren't like that.*"

But, she had to concede, many are. Far too many are. And since sexuality is central to the subordination of women, the increasing sexualization of women is … of concern. To understate.

But, well, women are no more immune to media influence than men. Why should we expect them to be?

Because they get such a bad deal when they buy it. They just don't know it. At first.

So why aren't women turning into feminists in droves, once they're treated like shit, or left with a child to raise, or turn forty?

Maybe they are. Maybe they are, but won't admit it, perhaps don't even recognize it.

Though men get a pretty bad deal too. It's just not as apparent. At first. Or ever. She knew men, too many men, who carried the macho burden on their backs well into old age. It was pathetic, really. Again, so little introspection, so little self-awareness …

*

"I can do whatever I want!" he blurted out when she returned to the room. "You're telling me I can't watch tv or play video games—but I can do whatever I want!" He sounded like a child.

Was it overcompensation for a domineering father? No, a domineering mother. Though in our society, *any* supervision of a male by a female is considered domineering. No matter the age difference. And the fact that it was a mother's *responsibility* to dominate, to provide supervision.

"You can go around hurting people? Stealing stuff, blowing up buildings—"

"That's not what I meant—"

"What did you mean then?"

He couldn't say. Of course he couldn't. So he just stared at her.

She waited for a few more moments, then tried another approach.

"This— None of this is *real* to you, is it. You're so used to posturing, you can't turn it off. In fact, I'll bet you've lost your real self, you've been posturing for so long. Who are you?" She looked at him. "What kind of person are you? What kind of life do you want?"

"What do you mean?"

"Take away all your friends. Imagine for a moment, it's just you. Imagine you hang out with no one but yourself. Do you like yourself? Is the person you are the person you want to be?"

He didn't know.

"What would your ideal life be like?" she continued. "Looking back, when you're fifty, what would you like to see?"

She'd once asked her boyfriend that very same question, and he'd responded with a litany of possibilities. It had been a purely intellectual response. He didn't *know* what he wanted.

Why was it so difficult for men? To know what they wanted. Because that would involve an assessment of their feelings? Which, apparently, were off limits? Not just to others but even to themselves? Real men don't feel. Neither pain *nor* pleasure.

No, she realized then, it wasn't that he didn't *know* what he wanted, it was that *he* didn't know what he wanted. Men don't have a sense of self. That's why they can't analyze themselves. They didn't *have* selves to analyze.

It would explain why they were so able to hurt others, to hurt other *selves*. How could they assume in the other what they themselves didn't have? Not just the capacity to feel, but a sense of self, a person with interests and aspirations ...

"Don't you care?" she pressed on. "About who you are?"

"Do I look like I care?"

"No," she sighed. "You don't." Without pain or pleasure, there's nothing to care about. "You look like you don't care about anything. In fact, you look like you *scorn* everything. And everyone. You look like you hold everything, and everyone, in *contempt*. Why is that?"

No answer.

"Do you think it makes you superior, better than other people, when you look down on them?"

Still no answer.

"It doesn't. It just makes you a fool. Because in most cases, there's no basis for such complete scorn, such complete contempt. Everyone has something praiseworthy about them.

"Well, "she corrected herself, "almost everyone."

He looked at her. A little hurt. Oh dear.

"And you look like you think that makes you a man. Not caring. About anything. I'll grant that's what society tells you. All the ads, all the pictures of men with no affect, their expressionless faces, their blank eyes—   They all look dead inside. You want to be like that?"

"What do you mean?"

She sighed. Again with the 'What do you mean?' She ignored it. Carried on.

"I mean you don't have to buy all the shit they feed you. About being a man."

Clearly, among the books he had *not* read were those by Stoltenberg and Jensen and—   Wait, just two? Was that all there were?

"You don't have to accept the limitations imposed upon you."

"What do you mean?"

"I mean you could think for yourself for one goddamned minute!" she shouted in exasperation.

She stood up and walked around the room for a minute.

Then she sat down and tried again. "*Why* don't you want to care? If you care, you can get hurt, I'll grant you that. But when you don't care, about women—and that seems to be integral to being a man—as you've so clearly demonstrated—you shut yourself off from half the human race. From so many people with whom you could have fun, adventure, friendship ... "

There was a flicker—

"And I'll grant you that many, perhaps most, of the women your age are just as bad. They too have been sexualized since birth. All the girls who fuss over how they look every minute of the day? Idiots. The ones who love to 'go shopping'? Airheads. The ones who want babies because that'll make them feel important? Suckers. The ones I hear guys refer to as 'high maintenance'—as if they're cars," she couldn't help adding, "that's what all the little princesses turn into."

He was listening.

"There are other girls out there. Not many, but some."

But he didn't believe her. Or didn't believe those other girls would ever—

And he was right.

So he shrugged. Didn't care.

"Okay then my question to you is 'Why are you still alive?' Why haven't you killed yourself out of sheer boredom? Are you a coward?"

He looked away.

"Are you just too lazy? Yeah, that's more likely," she said. "That's why you don't think. For yourself."

He started getting angry.

"And maybe you're a coward too, afraid of what you'll find. Afraid you'll figure out that you're responsible, for this, that you've done something wrong, something terribly wrong, that you owe someone—"

No. They were past apology.

She looked, really looked, at him. Forced him to look at her. "Don't you see? They've won. You've *already* killed yourself. They didn't have to do it, you did it yourself. You've become a hollow man, a shell, a zombie."

Is *that* why zombie movies are so popular, she suddenly wondered. They strike a chord of … recognition? God help us, validation?

"I did it because I did it, okay?" There.

"No!" she slammed her hand on the table. "I want to know *why* you did it."

"What do you mean?"

"I mean exactly what I said!" she replied with exasperation. "Which word don't you understand? 'Why' means—"

"I know what you mean!" he said angrily. Then slouched down in his chair.

"Then why did you ask me what I meant?" It was like talking to a teenager.

No, she corrected herself, she hadn't been anything like this when she was a teenager.

She got up and walked around the room again. After a minute or two, she returned to her seat.

"So, have you figured it out?"

"What do you mean?"

"Will you just stop that?! You didn't even *think* about what I said. You didn't even *try* to figure what I meant. Not that it takes much effort. I was pretty clear."

He just … stared at her.

"You say that a lot," she added. "'What do you mean?' At first, I thought you were doing it to buy time. To think of an answer to the question. But then you don't think. You don't answer the question.

"So now I'm thinking you do it to deflect the question. To throw it back on me. So you don't *have* to answer it. So you don't *have* to think."

Kept staring at her.

"And it's become habit, reflex. Not to think. Tell me, when was the last time you thought?"

"What do you mean?"

She groaned. "For the love of god— *Can* you think?"

The thought suddenly occurred to her: maybe he couldn't. "Are you mentally deficient?" she asked.

He just glared at her.

"I don't mean that as an insult. It's just— I'm beginning to wonder if you might be a bit retarded, since you're so unable to think. Have you been tested? Perhaps I'm asking too much of you. To develop insight into your own actions, your own motives."

"I'm not fucking retarded!" he shouted.

No, of course not. He attended university. She'd forgotten that for a moment.

"Then why are you so— Do you think that if you just drift through life, without thinking about anything, if you just let yourself be knocked about like a pinball, you won't be held accountable?" She held his gaze. "Well, guess what."

*

"It wasn't personal," he said when she returned to the room.

Well, he was right about that. Because neither one of them saw her, considered her, as a person. She was just a means to their ends.

And, or, because they were incapable of *being* personal. Because they'd denied, hadn't developed, any of the stuff that would make *them* persons. At the very least, individuality.

"I didn't mean to," he added. Whispered.

"Didn't mean to what?"

"Didn't mean to rape you." He looked at the door nervously.

"What did you mean to do, then?"

"I didn't mean to hurt you."

"Question still stands. What did you *mean* to do, then?"

"I don't know!" he wailed.

"How can you not know what you meant to do? Are you not conscious? Do you have no intent?"

"I don't know!" he repeated, though surely not in response to her last two questions. "I don't know what to say! Just tell me what to say!" he begged.

As if words, too, were merely instrumental. And not expressive of some ... truth.

"If you truly don't know what you meant to do, don't you think it's about time you figure it out? I'm not asking you why you went to a hockey game!" She spread out the photographs again. "Look at the blood! Look at the bruises! What was your *intent? Why did you do that to me?*"

Something as consequential as this cannot be done so ... casually, so thoughtlessly. It just can't.

"Isn't that ... normal?" he asked. "It's just rough—"

"NO!" she screamed as she stood up. Read some books, why don't you, or talk to—   He wouldn't have a girlfriend. And it wasn't the sort of thing he'd talk about with his mother or his sister. And when he and his friends talked about it, it would be exaggeration, fabrication. Or worse, not.

"You had to force me. Your buddy had to hold me down, smack me a few times. Don't you think that if it was normal sex, I would have been ... co-operating?"

He turned away.

"What exactly were you *meaning* to do," her words forced him to turn back, "when you rammed your penis into me, into my body, into my vagina—   Oh my god," she broke off, "you cringed when I said the word 'vagina'." Unbelievable.

"Are you uncomfortable with the word?" She stared at him. "How can you be uncomfortable with 'vagina' when that's what you rammed your penis into, again and again? What did you think you were ramming your penis into? Some warm and fuzzy place that totally had nothing to do with *me?*"

He turned away again.

"You rammed your penis *into my vagina.* Say it. Vagina. Va-gi-na. SAY IT!" she screamed.

"Vagina," he said. In a small voice.

"Say 'I rammed my penis into your vagina. Again and again.' SAY IT!" She was still on her feet, leaning across the table.

"I rammed my penis into your vagina again and again and *I'm sorry,* okay!?" But he'd said it with anger. Not with remorse. Because she had won.

She started pacing the room, trying to vent her rage.

"But he kept *pushing* me," he explained. Whined. "Said I was a loser, called me a girly girl, told me I had to grow up and be a man."

"And you just ... accepted his definition of 'a man'?" She stopped and turned to him.

He raised his shackled hands helplessly.

"And ... you decided that doing that," she returned to the table and pointed to the photographs, "was the lesser of two evils? You figured that for you to be called a loser, and a girly girl, was worse than for me to be beaten, and raped?" She let that sink in.

Then screamed at him, "How fucking fragile *are* you?"

He looked at her. Seemingly just now processing that implication of his decision.

"I'm sorry," he finally said. Repeated. Without the anger.

"Not good enough." She sat down. "Not by a long shot."

"And I feel just awful about it," he added. "Now that I know." He lifted sad puppy-dog eyes to her.

Oh for— He expected her to comfort him? Unfuckingbelievable. He'd managed to make it all about him. How *do* they manage to keep putting themselves in the center of the universe?

"I don't want an apology!" she stood up again as she screamed. "I want remediation! I want you to spend the rest of your life stopping other men from doing what you did! I want you to stand up to your friends, I want you to make new friends and stand up to them, I want you to speak in schools and universities, I want you to lobby for sentencing commensurate with the crime, I want you to raise the money required to test the DNA in the hundreds of thousands of rape evidence kits that are currently just sitting in labs across the country— I want you to make amends," she sat down. "For the rest of your life."

5

The following week, only the first one was brought into the room.

"You're the one who sodomized me," she said flatly. "Said you didn't want 'sloppy seconds'. Like I'm what, fast food?"

"Guess you haven't heard of that place in Germany. The King George. Serves 1.2 million per day," he grinned, then sang the McDonald's five-note jingle, "Ba da ba ba ba." And kept grinning.

She—

"Know what's on the menu?" he taunted. "'All-you-can-fuck.' For $135."

She saw that he wasn't kidding, saw that it was true, and threw up.

"Shit, why'd you do that!", he yelled as her vomit spilled onto the table, towards his shackled hands. "Get that shit away from me! GUARD!"

A million men a day. Serviced by how many women, she wondered.

There was probably a kiddies' menu you could ask about. She threw up again.

"FUCK!! GUARD! GET IN HERE!" He screamed again at the closed door.

She got a tissue from her bag, wiped her mouth, walked unsteadily to the door, knocked, then just … left. Fresh air. She needed some fresh air. Where was their fresh air?

*

An hour later—she'd googled the brothel he'd mentioned and discovered that anal fist fucking and even cutting a woman was also on the menu. *Legitimized* by *being* on the menu. No surprise then. When all women are hos …

A *long* hour later, when she returned, the table had been cleaned. The second one was still sitting there. Seething. Wordlessly, she sat down, then carefully set the photographs, one by one, in front of him. He looked away.

"You can't look? Is it too personal, a close-up of my rectum? But you forced your penis into it. It wasn't too personal then."

"Whatever." He shrugged with an exaggerated indifference.

"You find this *boring*? I'm sorry, is my pain too insignificant to hold your attention? Are the consequences of your action … tiresome?"

Of course he was bored. If you don't care about anything, you're not interested in anything.

"Why did you do it? Why did you force your penis into my rectum? Why did you hurt me in such a way?"

He shrugged again.

"You don't know? Don't you think you *should* know? We're not talking about why you went to a movie. Why—"

"What do you want me to say," he interrupted. "That I'm sorry? Okay, yeah. I'm sorry. Okay?"

"No. *Not* okay." Not by a long shot. There was simply no apology possible for what he'd done.

She waited.

"Try again," she finally prompted. "Why—"

"I don't know, okay!?" Would the bitch never leave him alone?

"Did you feel pressured to do it?" she asked. "And you were unable to resist that pressure?"

Certainly, he'd been pressured from birth to show contempt for women. He'd learned at an early age that to be called a girl, and therefore, to *be* a girl, was an insult.

And, apparently, he *was* unable to resist that, that lifetime of pressure.

But showing contempt was one thing.

"Or maybe you just enjoy hurting people. Maybe you just enjoy hurting women. Why?"

"I said I don't know!" he shouted. "I don't *have* a reason, okay?"

"So, what, you just walk around doing things for no reason? You have no conscious control over what you do? If that's true, who knows what you'll do next? Walk naked down the street singing showtunes? Buy an automatic and take out a classroom full of kids? Who knows?" she repeated, shrugging her shoulders with exaggerated helplessness. "Apparently not you!"

He glared at her.

"And if that's the case, you really should be locked up. For life. A prerequisite for being able to move freely among other people should certainly be the ability to control one's actions, don't you think? At the very least, a minimum level of rational behaviour. I mean, we can usually predict when a bear, for example, is going to attack someone. They have *reasons*: hunger, fear, defence of their young, self-preservation. But you're telling me you have *no* reasons. For anything."

He leaned back, tried to cross his arms on his chest before he realized he couldn't, then scowled at her. As if it were her fault he was shackled.

"I think you're just *pretending* not to have a reason, a motive, because you think that you can't be blamed then, you can't be held responsible. Do you really think that if you go through life denying agency, just going along for the ride— You're the fucking car! Take the wheel, god damn it!"

She got up and walked around. Only partly to show that she could. And he couldn't.

"Don't you think you *should* know?" she repeated. "Why you do the things you do?"

She returned to her chair. Sat down. Looked at him.

"And if you don't know, don't you think you should *figure it out?*"

She leaned back. Waited.

"So?" she asked after a minute. "Are you thinking? Are you trying to figure it out?"

"No," he huffed. "Why should I?"

"'Why should I?'" she repeated his question with mock thoughtfulness.

"Because consciousness separates humans from the other animals," she provided an answer. "Humor me. Prove you're at least one step up from a ... maggot."

He made his face blank.

"It's not innate knowledge I'm after, and it looks like you haven't thought about it. So think about it. Figure it out. I'll wait." She crossed her arms.

After a moment, she decided she'd better remind him what he was supposed to be figuring out.

"Figure out why you hurt women."

Still stone-faced. Clearly not thinking. About why he did what he did.

Why is there such a resistance to self-knowledge? She'd seen it in every man she'd ever known. Her father, her brother, her few boyfriends. It was as if they considered it a badge of honor *not* to be self-aware. Real men don't reflect.

Finally she got up again. "I'm taking another break. See if you can figure it out by the time I get back."

*

"So," she returned to the room, "have you figured it out?"

"What do you think?"

"I think not. It's hard. Thinking. It takes a strong person to think. And it takes an independent person to think for himself. I suspect you're neither. You're weak and, despite appearances, a follower. You follow the expectations of your buddies, and you follow the examples you see in movies, online games, porn.

"So, I'll help," she said. Cheerily.

She knew it would make him angry. To need help was bad enough. To need a woman's help was an insult. Pure and simple. Merely by offering her help, she had insulted him. No wonder. The world.

"Maybe someone hurt you and you want to hurt back. But you overgeneralize when you hurt me. I wasn't the one who hurt you. Do you understand?"

Silence.

"Maybe a woman hurt you. But if you hurt all women in return, again, still, you're overgeneralizing. It's like when a child is told that the family dog is a 'dog' and then points to everything with four legs and fur, saying 'dog'. That's overgeneralizing."

"I'm not a child!"

"Well, you're acting like one."

He glowered at her.

"Your buddy mentioned getting points. Is that why you did it?"

Maybe there were extra points for anal sex. Because the additional pain caused was proof of additional power. Over the other.

Or maybe— Sjoo and Mor suggest, in *Female Erasure*, that frontal, face-to-face, sex implies the personalization of sex; it would follow that anal sex implies the depersonalization of sex, the subordination, the degradation, of women *via* their depersonalization.

"Was it some sort of hazing?" she persisted. "Did you feel *obliged* to do it? Did someone *make* you do it?"

God help us, there was now a crime called 'compelled rape' in many countries.

"No," he snorted.

"No, of course not, no one makes you do anything. Because you think for yourself so well."

"Bitch."

"Oh, did that hurt? Was what I said a little humiliating? So is that wrong?"

He just … fumed.

"Look," she said, "I'm not one of those women who define themselves by their sexuality. In fact, I don't even identify myself as a woman. My sex is about as important to me as my eye colour.

"But apparently it's all that matters to the rest of the world. We're identified as girls or boys from day one. Pink and blue. Ms. and Mr.

"And apparently it's important to you. I'd go so far as to say it's *all* that's important to you. You see me *only* as a woman. A female. A sexual thing. A cunt.

"But even that … Well, it's nothing new, really. I've been dealing with that all my life."

She realized that, now.

"But after you pounded at me, into me, ripping me a little bit more each time, you came on my face. Why did you do *that?* It was humiliating. You humiliated me."

"Right." There was sarcasm in his voice.

"Are you implying that it's *not* humiliating? Being ejaculated onto? It's like being urinated on! That's not humiliating?"

"It's just what— It's part of—" He looked around as if he was so very put upon, having to explain this.

"Be nice if you could finish a sentence. Or two."

"It's what's done!" he shouted in frustration.

"Where? To who? And, again, *why?* How many times do I have to ask?"

"I DON'T KNOW, okay!?" he shouted.

"NO! It's NOT okay!" she shouted back. "FIGURE IT OUT!"

She glared at him.

"Figure out why you tore me apart! Why you contaminated the rest of my life! Every day of the rest of my life! I have flashbacks. I have fear. I have anger. Surely I'm entitled to know why!"

He stared at her. A little surprised.

Surprised?

A *little* surprised?

She couldn't leave her apartment anymore without thinking it could happen again. Who knew when a couple *other* guys would overwhelm her, hold her down, and *use* her. Like she was some *thing* to be *used*. Then dribbled on.

Brownmiller had said it, over forty years ago: "[Rape] is nothing more or less than a conscious process of intimidation by which all men keep all women in a state of fear."

Though maybe the incident—the *incident*—that's how people referred to it—maybe it had just ripped off her rose-coloured glasses. After all, one in three. She shouldn't have felt comfortable leaving her apartment in the first place. She should have been afraid and angry all along.

As should be all women. And girls. Females.

Oh god, they'd weaponized sex. They'd turned what could have been, what should have been …

*

"When you said 'It's what's done,' did you mean it's what's done in porn?" she asked when she returned yet again. "And you did it because the women in porn acted like they liked it? So you thought *I'd* like it?" They'd been here before, but.

He nodded. Just once.

"Then I've got a nice piece of property in Florida to sell to you."

It took him a moment. Then he glanced away.

"How would you feel if *you* were sodomized?" Been here before too, but.

He shrugged. Didn't seem to be trying to imagine it. Or perhaps couldn't.

"How would you feel," she persisted, "if someone held you down, ripped your pants off, and shoved a cucumber up your ass. Pushed it in, then pulled it out, pushed it in again, then pulled it out, in and out, in and out."

He squirmed. Just a bit.

"You'd scream, you'd squeal like a pig, but you'd *like* it—right?"

"That's a bit harsh," he finally said.

She burst out with a laugh of disbelief. Then stared at him. Silently urging him to see the irony.

After a long moment, she said, simply, "I don't believe you. Not for a second. I don't believe you thought I'd like it. Any of it. I don't know anyone who *would*. Would *you* like it if some guy shot his come all over your face?

"No, don't tell me," she anticipated, "it's different. Women are *supposed* to like being humiliated."

She looked at him evenly. "You are so fucked up."

He stood suddenly and towered toward her. "YOU DESERVED IT, BITCH!"

A guard appeared at the window. A woman this time. She glanced into the small room then moved on.

"Okay," she said, unperturbed, "finally we have a *reason*. And it even involves *justice*. Very good. Now. What did I do to deserve it?"

He remained standing. The vein in his temple stood out.

"I think you're overgeneralizing again," she said calmly. "Though, honestly, I'm not sure the woman you're confusing me with would have deserved it either."

"Look, I don't need this shit!" he sat down in a huff, needlessly clattering the shackles as he did so.

"It's not a question of what you need." Why did men always frame things that way? Oh, wait.

"I don't want to argue with you, okay?" What he meant was he didn't want to discover that his opinion on the matter was indefensible. Of course, he didn't know that's what he meant.

She ignored him. "Why—"

"As I said before, bitch," he glowered at her, "I was drunk."

"Yeah, but why did being drunk make you sodomize me? Instead of, say, dance the Macarena with me? You must have *wanted* to sodomize me. And being drunk just …"

"Yeah, that's it. I *wanted* to do it."

There. He'd said it. But she knew he hadn't meant it. At least he didn't *know* he'd meant it. Still a way to go. A long way.

No, hang on. She wasn't here for *him*. She wasn't here so *he* would understand. And so far, all *she* understood was that they did what they did because they thought women were less than human but they didn't even know that that's what they thought and/or didn't have a reason for thinking that. It was all very unsatisfying.

And no, that wasn't even— You can think something is less than human and still *not* hurt and humiliate it.

She was back where she started. Why did men hurt and humiliate women?

"I think you did it because you truly do hold women, all women, in contempt. So you like humiliating them.

"Furthermore, humiliating someone puts them beneath *you*. So that makes you one-up." Men would rather die than be a loser, and beating up women meant they weren't a loser.

Wait— How does beating up women mean you're *not* a loser?

He was listening. Maybe.

"But quite apart from the mistakes in logic—just because you hold someone in contempt, it doesn't follow that you should humiliate them, and humiliating someone doesn't make them beneath you, it just indicates that you *think* they're beneath you— Why do you hold *women* in such contempt? Why do you like humiliating *them?*"

Silence.

"Okay, one question at a time. What did I ever do to you to make you feel such contempt toward me?"

Wrong question. If he was generalizing. And honestly, she could understand why men held in contempt at least those women who expected them to pay their way. She herself held such princesses in contempt.

"Nothing." She answered the question anyway.

Then addressed the correct question. "It's what I *am* that upsets you. So I ask, why is it you feel such contempt for *women?* What is it about us that upsets you so much?"

"You don't upset me."

"Clearly we do. Or you wouldn't have such strong feelings about us."

He laughed with derision. "Said it before, bitch. I don't have strong feelings about you."

"Sure you do. You *despise* us. Why?"

He was silent.

"I want to know *why!*" she screamed in frustration.

Why do you watch porn? Why do you play those video games? Why do you refuse to vote for female political candidates? Why do you sabotage women working in traditionally male professions? Why do you boo when a woman gets the prize for the highest grades?

"You don't know. Of course you don't. My god, how can anyone be so clueless about themselves?"

"You're a fucking bitch! You're nothing but a cunt, you know that?"

And there it was. Prick the skin of any man and the misogyny bursts out. Like pus. Exactly like pus.

"Yeah, see, that's what I thought. You have complete and utter disdain for women. You hate us. And, or so, you see nothing wrong with hurting us, humiliating us. In fact, I think you enjoyed hurting me. I think maybe you were excited by my screams of pain. You certainly enjoyed coming on my face. So my question is, no surprise, *WHY?*"

Again, silence.

She got up. "Well, you keep trying to figure it out. I'll be back next week."

"You know what your problem is?" he said as she walked toward the door.

"Yeah." She turned. "You. And every man like you."

It seemed hopeless. She was to have no satisfaction. She might never be able to understand why he did what he did. Not because he didn't know why, but because there was no why. There was no reason.

This is why people become religious, she thought. To believe that everything happens for a reason. The alternative is almost unbearable. It takes courage to face the fact that so much pain is … pointless. Acknowledging, intellectually, that the universe is irrational is one thing; seeing, feeling such irrationality up close and personal is quite another.

Or rather, there was a reason, but it was so … impersonal. The core of the assault was a simple, but deep and possibly irremediable, contempt by men for women.

And why did men feel such contempt for women? Why would they spit on them, piss on them, ejaculate on them?

Because contempt for women was just part of the definition of being a man. As was, paradoxically, having sex with a woman; men who didn't 'get' sex were losers; didn't matter if it was by force; perhaps it was better if it was by force.

And most males had to be, just *had to be*, men. Just as most females had to be women. For what else could they be? To be a person, to identify oneself (let alone others) not by the accidental attributes one was born with, whether sex or skin color or nationality, but by the attributes one chose, the attributes one developed, well, that was a lot of work.

6

Next time, both of the men were in the room again. She sat in the chair opposite them. Again.

"So," she looked from one to the other, "have either of you figured it out? Why you did what you did?"

"We just did it," the first one says tiredly, "we didn't have a reason, okay? Give it up, already."

"Yeah," the second one followed suit.

She looked at the second one for a moment, then, ignoring their 'problem solved' implication, summarized. "We've established that you think women are solely sexual things available for your use. And that that somehow gives you the right to hurt and humiliate them. Have you figured out yet why you think that?"

Silence.

"No? Then perhaps you should *stop* thinking that, yeah? I mean if you don't have a good reason for your beliefs, your opinions—"

"We don't *need* reasons for our beliefs," the first one said with such … disdain.

"Okay, but then you have no right to act on the basis of those beliefs," she said. "Do you?"

A minute passed. Two minutes passed. "Well?"

"Well what?" The first one. With such belligerence.

"People who can't explain, can't justify, their beliefs shouldn't be allowed to act on those beliefs. I mean, I shouldn't be allowed to just go around and do stuff at random for no reason at all. Should I?"

"Wouldn't bother me none."

Quick as a snake, she stood up and smacked his nose. Broke it, in fact.

He screamed. And pulled at his shackles. In vain.

A guard appeared at the door. The same guard as before. No doubt her hand went to her sidearm, but she assessed the situation and decided that no intervention, no assistance, was needed at the moment.

"What the fuck?" the second one looked at her, alarmed. "Why did you do that?"

"Oh *now* you want reasons."

"YOU FUCKING BITCH!!" the first one was still screaming. At her now. His face was red with rage. And a bit of blood. If his hands weren't cuffed to the table, he would've lunged at her.

The way he'd said it made it sound like "Not fair!"

"What," she challenged, "I'm not entitled to retaliate? How do you figure that?"

Ah. When you're entitled to everything, without consequence, retaliation for exercising such entitlement violates that entitlement. So it isn't fair.

How did one develop that attitude, that belief, she wondered. She simply couldn't imagine ever feeling, let alone ever thinking, that she was entitled to … everything. To anything she wanted. Without consequence.

And since, when, men felt entitled to women, defence against sexual assault wouldn't be fair either. It would be getting in the way, interfering with his entitlement.

She smacked his nose again. His already broken nose.

He screamed again.

"What the hell are you doing?!" the second said in protest.

"Oh come on, quit your crying," she said to the first one. "You wanted that. You *liked* that. Men enjoy this sort of thing."

Once he'd recovered, somewhat, he looked at her levelly. It was almost the first eye contact he'd made. "When I get out of here, bitch," he said quietly, "I'm going to kill you."

She was unfazed. "Hm. Why? Oops. Another question you can't answer. Well, the same question, actually."

"I'M GOING TO KILL YOU BECAUSE I HATE YOU!!"

"Okay, now we're getting somewhere again. Why do you hate me?

"Follow-up, why do you want to kill people you hate?

"And, one more follow-up, on what basis do you think it's morally acceptable to kill people you hate?

"Can you remember those three questions?" she asked politely. "Maybe you should write them down. Because that's your assignment for next time. Figuring out the answers to why do you hate me, why do you want to kill people you hate, and on what basis is that morally acceptable. Got it?"

She was being so fucking patronizing.

And it felt so fucking good.

"But no, what would be the point? I'd come back next week, ask you if you'd figured it out, and again, you'd say no. Well," she qualified, "you wouldn't actually say no, you'd just glare at me. Refusing to admit you didn't know."

She paused.

"You don't know very much, do you. I don't think you know anything. I must've asked a dozen questions, but," she counted them off on her fingers, "you don't know why you hurt me. You don't know why you humiliated me. You don't know why you hate me. You don't know why you hate women. You don't know why you're so contemptuous of women. You don't know why you enjoy hurting women." She paused. "Why have you been unable to answer even *one* of these questions?"

His face darkened.

"I know!" she said brightly and included the second one in her gaze. "It's because you're *men*! Denial, excuse, deflection. That's your complete response repertoire. Even among yourselves. When a buddy accuses you of something, what do you do? You deny it! And if that doesn't work, you make excuses! Why can't you guys just take responsibility for your actions?

"It seems to me that men will do *anything* to avoid facing the truth. To avoid *figuring out* the truth. Even when it concerns you. Perhaps *especially* when it concerns you.

"Why are men so afraid of introspection?"

The second one spoke up. "We're not afraid—"

"Of *anything*, no. Got that. And yet you avoid it at all costs."

To be fair, a lot of women weren't terribly self-aware either. But they were tasked with relationship maintenance. Which required awareness of how both they, and the other person, were feeling.

Women were also tasked with child care. And despite its low status, being responsible for an infant, toddler, or child, and often all three at once, also required a very high level of awareness—again, not only of self but also of the other.

Of course, being tasked with something didn't necessarily mean you were good at it. But it did mean that at least you got more practice at it. And so were likely to be at least better at it than the person *not* so tasked.

Regardless, generally speaking, they weren't the ones sexually assaulting people.

*

"If you can't explain your actions," she said when she returned after a break, during which someone had come in and bandaged the first one's nose, "I'll have to do it for you."

She sighed. That's why Sweden, Norway, and other countries were so advanced compared to Canada and the States. They taught their kids how to think. They had philosophy in elementary school. So kids learned early on to establish reasons for their opinions, their actions. They weren't as dependent on emotion. And, so, they weren't as vulnerable to profit-motivated media, weren't as easily suckered in by the messages to do this, be that.

"I think that you meant to do exactly what you did. Partly because you're both morons and you don't think for yourselves, but instead do whatever our culture, or your subculture, tells you to do. Which includes pretty much anything that shows contempt for women. Because your status, as males—and that's the only thing your status depends on, your sex, because god knows there's nothing about you as individuals that would give you any sort of status, you've been too lazy to develop any remotely impressive abilities or attributes—your status as males depends on putting us down. That's why you came onto my face," she turned to the first one. "It turned me into a toilet."

"You're crazy, you know that, right?" the second one said, glancing at his buddy with a grin.

And there it was. The ultimate dismissal. 'You're crazy.' It was such a quick and thorough way to de-legitimize someone, to de-authorize them, to ensure that what they say isn't taken seriously.

"Right. Well, until you come up with a better explanation, you'll have to accept mine. Unlike you, I *have* thought about these things."

"Yeah, well," the first one said dismissively, "everyone's entitled to their own opinion."

In other words, 'Yeah, well, I don't know how to determine whose opinion is better, whose opinion is more supported by evidence and argument.'

Or 'I don't want to determine whose opinion is better—because it's probably not mine.'

She resumed her explanation.

"And partly you did what you did because you genuinely hate women. One, because, according to you, women are weaker than you. They're losers. And since you hate losing, you hate losers.

"Never mind that you *want* them to be weaker than you. Because then you're stronger. You want women to be beneath you because then you're on top. But then you hate them for *being* beneath you. Go figure.

"And you hate women because two, you're sexually attracted to us and that makes you feel like a puppet on a string. And since it's *especially* emasculating to be … controlled, as you see it, *by a woman,* you're *especially* angry about it. So you need to punish us. You need to punish women. Viciously. And sexually.

"But that's irrational too," she continued. "Because most of us? We're not baiting you. I certainly wasn't. Again, you're buying into the view of women that Hollywood and gaming shoves down your throat."

Kimmel astutely noted the way men described women's sexuality: 'She's a bomb-shell, she's dressed to kill.' As if *women* were doing violence against *men*.

"We are not evil demon seductresses, we're not sexy temptresses. Most of us are just trying to hang onto our jobs, pay rent …

"So you don't need to get back at us. You don't need to conquer us.

"We're not controlling you," she summarized. "Your own body's doing that. So if you hate anyone, hate yourself. Blame *your* body, not mine.

"And if you don't want to be driven by your body, then why don't you do something about it?"

"What, you want to castrate us all?"

Right. Of all the things she'd said. Because of course that was really the only thing men feared. As if their testicles were The Most Important Things in The World. And not just part of an involuntary delivery system of a non-conscious and therefore supremely stupid gene that was hell-bent on replication.

*

"What happened to you?" she asked the second one when she returned to the room after yet another break. "Last time we met … It's like when two or more of you are together, you turn into the borg, become part of a hive mind."

If men, and many women, were so unable to be introspective, it would follow that their self-consciousness would be pretty low.

And that would explain why their sense of self would be so weak. Why they'd be more subject to the herd mentality. Why gangs, tribes, teams, and nations were so important to them.

Resistance is futile.

"Why are you afraid of him? What's he got over you?"

"I'm not afraid of him." He looked over at his buddy nervously.

"Sure you are. Because the last time I was here, you seemed to … understand. A bit. You even apologized, remember?"

"You apologized?" the first one turned to him, laughing. "Dude, have *you* been pussywhipped," he laughed.

"I didn't apologize," the second one said quickly. Was he even aware that he was lying? Was the herd mentality completely derailing the rational part of his brain? It would explain why men who wouldn't, when alone, hit someone, found themselves bashing someone's head into a brick wall when they were part of a mob.

And two is enough to be a herd? Scary thought, that. Points to legislative revision of the freedom of association. For men, at least.

"Be a man!" the first one chided. "Have some initiative! Ya gotta step up and *take* what you want!"

"Whether or not you deserve it?" she asked. "Whether or not it's yours? If you don't deserve it, that's not fair. And if it's not yours, that's theft. You stole access to my body."

He snorted. Fair didn't concern him. Fair was for wusses.

"You know," the first one said then, casually, "speaking of initiative, we've already made a nice chunk of change from the video." He leaned back. A smug look on his face.

What? They'd made a video? And— The blood rushed from her head, and she felt a wave of dizzy nausea.

He nodded the answer to her unspoken question. "Uploaded it to HotSex dot Com."

Her humiliation was online for everyone to see.

Her pain, and her humiliation, was … entertainment.

"We get half every time someone clicks on it."

They'd used her body for money. Of course they did.

"Don't you think I should get a cut?" she tried to speak their language.

"Why? *We're* the ones who recorded it. *We're* the ones set up the account and uploaded it."

"But—"

"You just lay there. Didn't even give either one of us a blowjob."

She— She just—needed a moment. She needed—

"Did you at least blur my face?" She had to know.

"Hell no! What happens on your face is sometimes the best part!" He grinned broadly.

7

The following week, both men were again in the room when she arrived. And when she arrived—it was the female guard who had passed her through the security check this time, after giving her an odd look—they both saw the swell at her belly.

"You got knocked up?" the first one snickered.

Knocked up. Must they turn *everything* into violence?

And snickered. Men shouldn't be allowed to impregnate anyone until they can treat pregnancy with respect, dignity, and appropriate emotion. To borrow Sarkeesian's words.

She took her seat at the table, setting her heavy bag beside her on the floor.

"Yes," she said then. And stared at him. "You were there. Your buddy 'knocked me up'. Don't you remember? Have you suffered a brain injury?"

It was the epitome of male privilege. Sex without consequences.

"You *do* know how babies are made, don't you?" She looked at one and then the other.

The first one smirked. The second one— A little discomfort crept onto his face.

Then, since neither one had actually said 'Yes' …

"There are sperm in your ejaculate—your cum, your jizz—and when you put it in a woman's vagina, they make their way into her Fallopian tubes. If there's an egg there—"

"We know about … the birds and the bees!" the second one said angrily.

"Then why are you surprised?"

Silence.

"Did you think that when it's rape, the woman suddenly develops voluntary control over fertilization? Implantation? Or that her body somehow erects a barrier? Spontaneously produces a spermicide?"

Wouldn't that be nice.

"Did you think the odds were against it? Rape results in 32,000 pregnancies per year." And stealthing— she'd recently discovered the word; it referred to the man taking off the condom part way through, without the woman's knowledge—who knew how many pregnancies that resulted in? Let alone infections with who knows what.

She'd been horrified to read about the practice. So prevalent it had a name. It had online communities of men talking about how to get away with it. 'Women have no right to make sexual decisions about their bodies,' it so much as said. 'What they want is utterly irrelevant.'

More silence.

"You don't know why you're surprised? Well, take a moment and figure it out. You really should understand why you feel the emotions you do," she said with cheerful encouragement. "I'll wait."

Minutes passed.

"Have you figured it out yet?" she asked the second one. "Why you're surprised that you made me pregnant?"

The first one was amused to see his buddy on the hot spot.

"Have you had a vasectomy? That would explain your surprise. Or maybe you have a very low sperm count. Is that the case?"

He was silent.

"*Have* you had a vasectomy?"

He made a sound.

"What does that mean? Please, use your words. I don't understand grunts. Have you had a vasectomy?" she repeated.

"No!" he shouted, angrily.

"Okay, there's no need to get angry! Why does the question make you angry?"

More silence.

She knew, of course. Men pride themselves on their reproductive ability. God knows why, because once they reproduce, they don't pride themselves on their caretaking ability. It was evolutionary psychology gone mutant. Because surely taking care of one's spawn increased the chance that one's genes would survive as much as engaging in the sexual intercourse that produced said spawn. Irrational to the core, men were.

"You don't know? You don't know very much, do you? *Now* you don't know how sex works, you don't know why you're surprised, you don't know why you're angry ..."

"I know how sex works!"

"Then why are you surprised?"

"Because we were just fooling around—"

What? They considered what they did to her to be just *fooling around?*

They considered *creating a new human being* to be *just fooling around?*

No, of course not. What people meant when they said they were just fooling around was that they shouldn't be held responsible for their actions.

She rummaged in her bag, then set a piece of paper onto the table and pushed it across to the second one.

"What's this?" he glanced down at it.

"An invoice for my incubation services to date."

He read it, then looked up at her as if she was insane. "I'm not paying this!"

"Of course you are. Wait—did you expect me to provide my services for *free*? To *you*? Why in god's name would you think that?" She acted truly perplexed.

No response.

She persisted. "If you had no intention of paying for a pregnancy, why did you make one happen?"

"I *didn't* make one happen!"

"There are sperm in your ejaculate," she started the explanation again, "and when you put it in a woman's vagina—"

"Just shut up! Just shut the fuck up!"

"It's extra points," the first one spoke up. Gleefully.

"What?" She turned her attention back to him.

"It's extra points if you do it without a condom."

Even this, they turned into competition. No surprise, really.

"Why?" she asked. "Because then you'd be *really* screwing me? Fucking up *the rest of my life* with a kid I can't afford, a kid I don't want?" Unbelievable.

She suddenly realized why 'Fuck you' was an insult. To fuck someone—to impregnate someone—was to destroy them. Their hopes, their dreams, their aspirations. Their autonomy.

She turned to the second one. "What did I ever do to you? Why do you hate me so much you want to … derail my life?"

No response.

"And how sick do you have to be to do that by using, making, a new human being?"

"I—"

"Oh, wait," she beat him to it. "You don't know."

"I guess I thought you'd do something," he said finally. A slight challenge in his voice.

"You *guess* you thought *I'd* do something. Why should *I* be the one to do something? I was forced into this, remember? By you! So doesn't that make it *your* responsibility?" she added.

"I just figured you'd do something," he repeated.

"Could you be more specific?"

He glared at her.

"What now? You don't *want* to be more specific? Why don't you want to be more specific? You know, for someone who's so cavalier about having sex, you're astonishingly incapable of talking about it."

"I thought you'd take care of it!" he nearly shouted.

"'Take care of it.'" Meaning … *not* take care of it.

"Yeah, I thought you'd get rid of it."

"'Get rid of it.'" She repeated those words too. "Like it's a piece of garbage? An old couch?"

She stared at him.

"So you thought you'd rape me, make me pregnant, and then I'd get an abortion. Okay, did you have any particular clinic in mind? Do you know how much they charge? Do you know how long their waiting list is?"

"I thought you were on something."

Well, which was it?

"'On something.' You mean contraception? And risk cancer, stroke, and heart disease? Just so a man can have sex with me without a condom? Not likely. Why would you think that?"

No answer.

"Don't you think you should've asked? To be sure? I mean, this is pretty ... substantial. You've created a new human being. That's a lot to be responsible for. Oh wait, you're not responsible for it. You're not responsible for anything."

"It's your body," the first one said then. Smugly.

The woman looked at him, calmly. Before she screamed—

"THEN KEEP YOUR FUCKING HANDS OFF IT!"

The guard appeared at the door, assured herself that the men were still shackled, then turned away.

"By the time I realized I was pregnant, it was too late," she said. "When I missed my period—" she saw them both look away. "Oh,

I'm supposed to be comfortable with *your* bodily fluids, but you're—you're actually *squirming.* My god, GROW UP!" She glared at them.

"When I missed my period," she resumed, "I thought it was because of the trauma."

The first one snorted.

"What, you don't think I was traumatized? Having one man hold me down while the other rapes me? Being sodomized? Being punched—"

"We didn't punch you."

That's where they draw the line? Right. Because rape isn't assault. It's just sex.

"You slammed part of your body into mine, over and over and over," she said. Isn't that punching?

"And," she added, "you slapped my face, hit my jaw a couple times."

"Yeah, to shut you up."

"Oh, did my screaming annoy you?"

"Yeah." He grinned. "You were all hysterical."

She took a breath. And another.

Finally, quietly, "You have *no* comprehension of what it is you've done. For that alone, you should be locked up. You're like a two-year-old in an adult male body. Both of you.

"You were *tearing my rectum!*" she screamed at the first one. "Do you know what that feels like? Have you ever had your rectum torn?

"And you," she turned to the other one, "you were tearing my vagina! And you were quite possibly making me pregnant!

"And," she looked back and forth, "you were possibly giving me herpes, venereal warts, AIDS, gonnorhea, syphilis, god knows what—"

"We don't have any of that shit."

"And I knew that how?"

They stared at her.

"When was the last time you were tested? For any of that shit?"

No response.

"Because surprise. You *do* have some of that shit."

She gave them a minute.

"Good thing, then, that I'm *not* pregnant." She reached under her sweatshirt and removed a pillow. "I would've started showing months ago. Morons."

*

"You wanna talk consequences?" the first one said as soon as she returned. "Because of you, we're both going to have criminal records!"

It took a moment. During which she thought of all the golden boy athletes who may have lost their scholarships because some awful bitch reported their sexual assault. And of Brock Turner's father who, according to a *New York Times* article, was upset that his son had lost his appetite as a result of his trial. Poor boy couldn't even enjoy a nice rib-eye steak fresh off the grill anymore.

"Because of *me*? How do you figure that?"

"You reported us."

"Because you committed a crime! *You* committed a *crime*. *That's* why you're going to have a criminal record!"

He looked away.

"Why is your well-being more important than mine?" she asked. Since that was, apparently, what he thought. "Why is your future more important than mine?"

"What's done is done. This doesn't affect your future."

"The hell it doesn't!"

"You said yourself you're not pregnant!"

"That's not the only— Do you have any idea how long it'll take before I can have sex without flashbacks to the pain and humiliation?"

He stared at her. She saw that what she'd said hadn't really registered.

"You honestly don't think that what you did was wrong, do you?"

Silence.

"Even a six-year-old would think otherwise. So what *the hell* is wrong with you?" she shouted, trying to get through his thick skull, his impenetrable acceptance of masculinity. Despite its pathological core.

She was a fool to expect any change. Not in just a few weeks. They didn't have the disposition. They didn't have the skills. The last time they thought about right and wrong was before puberty. Before testosterone flooded their bodies and shoved their brains off-line. From that point on, everything men did and said was focused on competition: one-upmanship, saving face. Winning precluded any attention to truth and good and right.

And it was best done with violence.

And women.

"What you did," she said, "was sexual torture." She knew that it had been a mild version of what was being done that very minute to god knows how many of the 4.5 million victims of sex trafficking. Her ordeal had lasted under an hour. And when it was over, she was let go.

"It was a hate crime." Ninety-eight percent of those victims were female. That was the reason they were victims. Worldwide, if you're female, and between 15 and 44, you're more likely to be injured or killed by a man, than by disease, war, and traffic accidents. Combined.

"She's right," the second one said to his buddy. "We *did* hurt her. We *did* do something wrong."

Wait, what? Women of the world, are you on your feet with cheers and applause? Are you, everywhere, dancing in the street? No. Not yet. Not nearly yet.

"Oh *now* you want to try to convince your buddy it was wrong," she looked at him. "Too late."

Still, the second one looked at her, begging for …

"What, you want me to thank you? Congratulate you, maybe? Oh my, aren't we a special little snowflake."

Then his expression registered.

"You want *forgiveness!?*" Unbelievable. "Why should I forgive you? Because that's what women do? They forgive the men who hurt them? Well, fuck that.

"Though I'm not sure I blame you," she said after a moment.

Relief flooded his face. It would be temporary.

"If I had that much testosterone coursing through my body, maybe I wouldn't think of anything but sex either. If the sexual urge is so great you call it a need, how do you men get anything done? With that constant undercurrent, that constant undertow …"

Though many studies show that men who rape do *not* have higher than normal levels of testosterone …

"And if I could just go and get me some, maybe I would. Maybe I wouldn't be able to resist the ever-present temptation. Especially if I fed it by watching porn."

And then it occurred to her. "Maybe the question isn't why you did this. Maybe the question is why you don't do it more often.

"Then again," she said, "I do blame you. Because even with that insistence relentlessly drumming in your brain, all you have to do is spend most of your day jerking off. Intercourse isn't necessary. That's meeting a different ... So yeah, changed my mind. I do blame you. For the rape. For the sodomy.

"And for not getting yourself fixed."

It took only a moment.

"See? She does want to castrate us," the first one said to the second one.

"Have you ever heard of a burdizzo?" she asked. "It's a clamp that essentially breaks the blood vessels leading to the testicles. Without blood, the testicles don't develop. So once you hit puberty, you wouldn't get that ... testosterone tsunami. The animals it's used on are calm, good-tempered, easy to get along with. They don't fight each other. And they still grow up to be big, beautiful, and healthy."

"We're not animals."

"I beg to differ," she said. An understatement if there ever was one.

"Even so, we have evidence that it would work the same way in humans. We've had cases in which the pituitary gland doesn't produce testosterone. Those men report feeling no urge to be violent. When they start receiving testosterone injections, they do.

"Consider testosterone gels, patches, caps. Don't they all increase aggression?

"I could be wrong, of course. But then, this isn't exactly my responsibility, is it. Fixing you. It's *your* responsibility. So *you* do the research. *You* figure it out."

Right. Like that's gonna happen.

"'Course, the problem isn't *solely* physical. But even there … The two of you don't appear to have been smart enough or critical enough or strong enough to have resisted the socialization you've been exposed to all your life. The millions of messages saying that women are inferior, they exist for your use, etc., etc., etc. The porn and the games that sexualize violence toward women.

"You said earlier that you can do whatever you want," she looked at the second one, "but you're giving up your ability to do just that. You're letting yourself to be turned into Pavlov's dog. Do you know about Pavlov's dog?"

"Yes, we know about Pavlov's dog," the first one said. "How stupid do you think we are?"

She let the question hang there a moment.

"You're still voluntarily exposing yourselves to such messages," she said. Pointedly. "You're like a kid who's been fed nothing but junk food all his life and so, then, finds himself at eighteen grossly overweight. As an adult, he finally understands why. But keeps on eating junk food.

"The analogy falls apart a bit, because I don't think you do understand why you are the way you are. You've demonstrated a complete resistance or inability to be introspective."

She got up and started walking around the room.

"Ideally, of course, we'd prohibit those messages. We'd change the socialization. In case nurture *can* trump nature. It seems able to do so, for a number of men. Though of course we don't know if those men have a less interfering nature. Less testosterone, for example.

"But addressing socialization would require massive regulation. Of the toy industry, for starters. And the porn industry, of course. And every single media stream … Regulation that would prohibit linking violence with fun, linking violence with excitement, *sexual* excitement …

"And, well, what do we do with the parents hell-bent on teaching their little boys to 'grow a pair', to 'be a man'? We could, of course, just prohibit them from reproducing. Reproducing their genes, reproducing their lies. To impressionable children. Who are never taught the skills needed to critically evaluate those lies."

Right. Like any of that would *ever* happen.

She saw the female guard standing near the door as she passed by.

"In the meantime," she started to suggest something, then reconsidered. "No, even if you stopped eating junk food, right now, completely … Developmental psychologists tell us that there are critical windows, during which certain changes can occur, but in your case, those windows closed long ago. It's too late for you two."

"You can't teach a dog new tricks," the first one agreed. Rather happily.

"Oh this wouldn't be a new trick," she said, taking her seat again. "It'd be a whole new way of seeing. Me. Yourself. And it would require nothing short of a whole new … theory of everything. And, to be blunt, you're not up to it.

"All of which is to say, I don't think the remedy lies in addressing the psychosocial or cognitive part of the problem."

They waited.

"Which leaves us with all that testosterone. Ten times what I've got. So no wonder."

The first one nodded. "We can't help ourselves," he said, grinning.

"Then you shouldn't be allowed the freedoms you have. Freedom of movement. Freedom of association. You shouldn't be allowed to hold any position of power.

"Furthermore, if it's the testosterone that's making you so aggressive toward women, so contemptuous of women, then you should put yourselves on testosterone inhibitors. Or estrogen supplements. To compensate."

Right. Like *that's* gonna happen.

"Because clearly you've got more testosterone coursing through your body than you can handle, more than you have the strength to resist. It's screaming at you all day and all night to FUCK! FUCK! FUCK! FUCK! FUCK! FUCK! and so you do.

"'Course, that wouldn't explain rape. Unless the testosterone is also saying HURT! HURT! HURT! HURT! Or maybe just FIGHT! FIGHT! FIGHT!

"Or maybe it's not the testosterone per se, maybe your brain is wired wrong, maybe you're just 'sick in the head'. Normal, yes, but also sick. You like to hurt others. You get off on causing others pain.

"Either way, it's obvious that your body is controlling you. Instead of vice versa.

"Which need not be a fatal flaw, but introspection is prerequisite for self-control, and you refuse to engage in introspection. It's like you don't *want* to know anything about yourself. Don't want to face the ugliness, I suppose.

"But even if you *had* the self-knowledge—which you should have now, at least a little bit—I'm not convinced you're strong enough … It seems you've also got the pull of the herd to resist.

"Or maybe you're just that weak-willed.

"It's not just you," she hastened to add. God knows why. "Put bluntly, men in general aren't as strong as they like to think. Nor are they in control as much as they like to think."

"So," she tried to wrap up, to summarize, "you can't have it both ways. Either you *can* control your sexual and/or aggressive desires—and I note that the 'and/or' might be wrong, because maybe they're one in the same, for men—in which case you *are* responsible for your actions, because you could have chosen otherwise. In which case you should stay here, in prison, for the rest of your life, because we don't want you out in the world choosing to rape and sodomize other women.

"Or you *can't* control yourself, in which case you *aren't* responsible for your actions. In which case we should take over. Control you. Either by keeping you here, again, for the rest of your life, or by one of the other methods I've mentioned.

"'Course, in the second case, perhaps the honorable thing to do would be to recognize that you're not in control and kill yourself. Hope you get a do-over with a body that doesn't force you to hurt other people."

She waited.

"So. Which is it? What's it gonna be?"

They stared at her.

"Well, okay, I guess that's the answer. If you can't even make *this* choice, I guess you *aren't* in the driver's seat."

She stood up. "Okay then. I know what my recommendation is going to be."

She headed toward the door.

"Wait—" the second one said. In a small voice. "What—"

"I'm going to recommend to the court that you be put on testosterone inhibitors. See whether—"

"BITCH!!" The first one strained at his cuffs.

"Woh," she paused at the door. "It's just a recommendation." There she was, appeasing again. "Based on my analysis. Do you have a better analysis? Of the problem? The solution? You haven't even figured out yet why you did what you did!"

She knocked and the guard opened the door. Stood in the doorway and nodded briefly to the woman.

"You know," she turned back to the first one, "it's interesting that my having just this little bit of influence over you—control, if you will—has you so enraged. You can hold me down, render me unable to move, inflict injuries with long-lasting side-effects, and you," she looked at the second one, "can force your sperm into me, make me endure nine months of pregnancy then labour then motherhood, or an abortion, or at least the morning-after pill," she looked back to the first one, "but I can't even *make a recommendation* about your future? How do you figure that?"

No response.

"And if this is how angry you get when a woman has even *that* little bit of power over you, well, that just *justifies* my recommendation, doesn't it."

She turned to the door again, but then realized she'd forgotten something. She walked back to the table for the pillow and her bag.

"What's that smell?" the first one wrinkled his nose.

"Oh. The consequences of your actions. *One* of the consequences of your actions," she corrected. "You tore my rectum, remember? So I'm on stool softeners. That way, bowel movements don't hurt as much. But it's kind of like having diarrhea," she grimaced.

"And, until my sphincter regains its elasticity, well, sometimes I just … leak. Smells like that's what's happened. I need to change my underwear."

She reached into her bag, then bent over and started to change her underwear.

They both bellowed objections and turned away.

"No need to turn away," she said. "You've seen all this before. Besides," she added, "have the courage to face what you did."

She stood up then, and with a slight grin on her face, flung her heavily soiled underwear at the first one. It landed on his head and hung down onto his face.

He screamed. So much so, you'd think she'd flung acid at him.

But since his hands were shackled, he couldn't do anything. He couldn't even wipe his face.

"FUCKING BITCH!!" His face was red with rage. He shook his head, trying to dislodge the soiled underwear. But that just made it worse.

"YOU BITCH, YOU FUCKIN' CUNT, I'M GOING TO KILL YOU!!"

"Yeah." Heard you the first time. And the second. And the third. And—

So next time, another time, she thought, it might *be* acid.

Or not.

Because then suddenly—no, it wasn't sudden at all—everything went black.

And a single shot sang out.

Or maybe it was two.

* * *

Or not.

9 781926 891774